MAX & the MILLIONS

ALSO BY ROSS MONTGOMERY

Alex, the Dog and the Unopenable Door

The Tornado Chasers

Perijee & Me

MAX & the MILLIONS

Ross Montgomery

WENDY
LAMB
BOOKS

Text copyright © 2018 by Ross Montgomery
Jacket art copyright © 2018 by David Litchfield

All rights reserved. Published in the United States by Wendy Lamb Books,
an imprint of Random House Children's Books, a division of Penguin Random House LLC,
New York. Simultaneously published by Faber & Faber Limited, London, in 2018.

Wendy Lamb Books and the colophon are trademarks of Penguin Random House LLC.

Visit us on the Web! rhcbooks.com

Educators and librarians, for a variety of teaching tools,
visit us at RHTeachersLibrarians.com

Library of Congress Cataloging-in-Publication Data
Names: Montgomery, Ross (Fiction writer), author.
Title: Max and the millions / Ross Montgomery.
Description: First edition. | New York : Wendy Lamb Books, an imprint of Random House
Children's Books, 2018. | Summary: Max discovers an entire, living world on the floor of the
bedroom of the eccentric janitor who disappeared from his boarding school, and must protect it
from the evil headmaster.
Identifiers: LCCN 2017006909 (print) | LCCN 2017033753 (ebook) |
ISBN 978-1-5247-1886-2 (ebook) | ISBN 978-1-5247-1884-8 (trade) |
ISBN 978-1-5247-1885-5 (lib. bdg.) | ISBN 978-1-5247-1887-9 (pbk.)
Subjects: | CYAC: Models and modelmaking—Fiction. | Size—Fiction. | Supernatural—Fiction. |
Hearing impaired—Fiction. | People with disabilities—Fiction. | Boarding schools—Fiction. |
Schools—Fiction. | Orphans—Fiction.
Classification: LCC PZ7.M76847 (ebook) | LCC PZ7.M76847 Max 2018 (print) | DDC [Fic]—dc23

The text of this book is set in 13.25-point Dante MT.
Interior design by Ken Crossland

Printed in the United States of America
10 9 8 7 6 5 4 3 2 1
First Edition

Random House Children's Books supports the First Amendment
and celebrates the right to read.

To Fred:
One small thing can save the world—
no pressure.

CHAPTER 1

Mr. Darrow was building a world.

He was building it in his bedroom, which was the biggest in the boardinghouse. The room was as cold and bare as a basement, with high ceilings and uncarpeted floors. Mr. Darrow had asked to be moved somewhere better, but the headmaster had always refused. After all, the headmaster would say, you're just a janitor.

Mr. Darrow wasn't *just* anything. He was a genius. Unfortunately nobody knew it but him.

After tonight, *that* was all going to change.

Mr. Darrow gazed at the miniature world on his desk. It was a little tray of sand, no bigger than a book. Inside were hundreds of tiny palm trees, each one made by hand and the size of a matchstick. They'd been planted in a ring around a green lagoon. It glimmered in the lamplight like an emerald dropped on the sand.

There was no doubt about it—this was Mr. Darrow's masterpiece. The greatest model he had ever made.

Other models filled the shelves above his desk. There were hundreds of them, piled on top of each other from floor to ceiling. Model boats, model planes, model palaces, monuments, dinosaurs, skyscrapers . . . each one smaller and more perfect than the last.

But they were *nothing* compared to his latest creation. It was paradise . . . and it was almost complete.

There was just one thing left to do.

Mr. Darrow opened a drawer beside him and took out a pair of metal goggles. They had two thick lenses and were covered in switches and wires. He pulled them on and pressed a button on the side. The lenses shot out like telescopes.

Mr. Darrow was proud of his microscope goggles—after all, he had built them himself. They were priceless.

Just like the serum.

Mr. Darrow picked up the tiny bottle beside him and held it up to the light. Less than a thimbleful of liquid lay inside, but the colors shifted and clouded in a pattern of millions. Mr. Darrow carefully swirled the bottle, merging red, then green, then blue, before the colors separated again.

It had taken him twenty years to find the serum. He never expected to get his hands on so much, and of such *perfect* quality . . . but even so, he had only one chance to use it.

He tilted the lamp over the sandbox. The lagoon shimmered.

"Light and water," he whispered. "That's all it needs."

Mr. Darrow swallowed. Five years of construction, twenty years of planning—it had all come down to this one moment. He tried not to think about what would happen if he used too much serum, or too little, or— and it didn't even bear thinking about—he dropped the bottle.

Mr. Darrow unscrewed the lid, took a deep breath, and leaned over his greatest work.

"Oh well," he said. "Here goes nothing."

CHAPTER 2

The headmaster cleared his throat.

"Good morning, children."

"Good morning, Mr. Pitt," replied five hundred voices.

Mr. Pitt smiled. The whole school was completely in his hands. He could tell them to start jumping up and down if he wanted to, and they'd do it. It was his favorite part of being a headmaster. That, and the speeches.

"Today," he announced, "is the last day of school. It is also the end of my first year as your new headmaster! While I've only been running St. Goliath's Boarding School for a short time, I feel like I've already gotten to know each one of you personally."

This was a lie. Mr. Pitt had spent the whole year in his office and still knew hardly any of the children's names, unless by coincidence they were all called Oi You.

"In an hour's time, the summer holidays will begin.

While you will all return home, I will be staying behind to oversee the next exciting stage in St. Goliath's history: the Pitt Building!"

He swept a hand toward what used to be the football pitch. It was now a building site, cordoned off with red tape. Five hundred children watched mournfully as a gang of builders tore out the goalposts.

"We will all miss the football pitch," said Mr. Pitt. "But as your headmaster it is my duty to bring this school into the *future*."

Some children asked if that meant there'd be cyborg teachers. Mr. Pitt gave them detention.

"It doesn't mean cyborg teachers," he said. "It means cutting-edge technology. State-of-the-art facilities. A brand-new school building to replace the old one."

He pointed to the school behind him and grimaced. St. Goliath's had been falling apart when he first arrived, and now it looked even worse. It was just one of the many things Mr. Pitt had assured the school governors he would change—along with abolishing free lunches, dismantling the library . . .

And, of course, getting rid of Mr. Darrow.

Mr. Pitt smiled. That was *one* thing off his list already—and he hadn't had to lift a finger.

"Which brings me to a sad piece of news." He gave a carefully rehearsed sigh. "I'm sorry to announce that yesterday our much-beloved school janitor, Mr. Darrow, has . . ."

Mr. Pitt trailed off. His eyes had been scanning the front row to measure the effect of his dramatic sigh, but now they stopped on a single chair. This one was different from the others. It said SPECIAL SEAT on the back in big red letters—so everyone could see—and it was empty.

Mr. Pitt looked up.

"Where's Max?"

CHAPTER 3

Max was hiding in a cupboard.

He usually hid in the bathroom, but they'd all exploded that morning—again—and Mr. Darrow still hadn't fixed them. St. Goliath's Boarding School was *filled* with things Mr. Darrow hadn't fixed.

Max was hiding for two reasons. First, because he didn't want to be at Mr. Pitt's speech. They'd make him sit in the SPECIAL SEAT again, like they did every assembly. Max didn't want to be the center of attention— he just wanted to be left alone so he could work on his models.

Which was the *second* reason he was hiding.

His castle was almost complete. It was small—no bigger than a jam jar—but there were more than a hundred rooms inside. It had towers with turrets and lockable doors and spiral staircases. Max had built them all himself.

"Here's where King Max will address his loyal subjects

each morning," he muttered, carving the final flourishes on the tallest tower. "And *here's* where he'll gather his knights each evening to share tales of battles past. . . ."

He took another scalpel from the kit in his lap and carved three tiny letters into the tower's base.

MAX

He smiled—the castle had taken him all term, but it was worth it. He couldn't *wait* to see the look on Mr. Darrow's face when he showed it to him and . . .

The cupboard opened.

"Max?"

Max looked up. There was a boy standing in front of him. He was the same age as Max, and wearing the same uniform, but that was where the similarities ended. This boy was taller, and cooler, and had a better haircut. Max hid the castle.

"Sasha! What are you doing here?"

"Looking for you!" said Sasha. "I thought the dorm was empty, but then I heard you in here talking to yourself. Oh—and I saw your headlamp."

Sasha pointed to Max's headlamp, which was a flashlight tucked into a pair of underpants worn over his head. Max switched off the light.

"It was dark," he mumbled.

Max clambered out of the cupboard and into the dorm he shared with Sasha. It was split perfectly down the middle. On Max's side were shelves of sci-fi and fantasy books, neatly arranged in alphabetical order. On Sasha's side were posters of a baseball team Max had never heard of, and hundreds of photos of Sasha with all his friends back in America.

"So why are you still here?" asked Sasha. "Everyone's listening to Mr. Pitt's speech! Didn't you hear the announcement?"

Max fumbled. "Oh! The speech! Er . . ."

"Wait!" said Sasha. "I get it . . . your ears, right?"

Max blinked. "My ears?"

"Your hearing aids."

Sasha pointed to the plastic tubes round Max's ears. Max bristled.

"No, actually, my hearing aids didn't have *anything* to do with . . ."

Max stopped. He hated being the only deaf child at St. Goliath's. He hated the way he was made to sit in the SPECIAL SEAT at the front of assemblies, and he hated the way everyone spoke to him IN A BIG LOUD VOICE even though that made it harder for him to follow what they were saying . . . but he realized that this was one of the times when being severely deaf could be severely useful.

"I mean . . . *yes*, you're right," said Max. "I didn't

9

hear the announcement. My hearing aids must have . . . stopped working."

Sasha beamed. "Hey! That reminds me!"

He held out his index fingers and crossed them over each other, like they were hugging.

"I looked it up on the Internet! Cool, huh?"

Max was confused. "What is it?"

"It's sign language!" said Sasha. "It means 'friend'— right? Am I doing it wrong?" He paused. "Wait—I must have looked up *American* Sign Language! You use *British* Sign Language over here, right?"

Max blushed. "Er . . . I don't know. I don't use sign language."

Sasha's face fell. "You don't?"

"I never learned."

Sasha let his fingers fall apart. There was an awkward pause.

"Well . . . better get going!" he said. "Don't want to miss the end of the speech!"

The two boys made their way through the boarding-house in silence. All their conversations ended like this. They might have shared a dorm—all students at St. Goliath's had to—but as far as Max was concerned, that was the only thing he and Sasha had in common.

Sasha had arrived from America at the beginning of the year, and in less than a week *everyone* knew who he was. The reasons were obvious: he was friendly and out-going, with expensive clothes and a slick accent. You'd always see him walking around school in the middle of a big group, chatting away confidently. He did everything with confidence—he could probably juggle pineapples in a nightgown, and he'd still look cool while doing it.

Max, on the other hand, was *not* cool. He knew he wasn't, and he didn't need any reminding about it, thank you very much. He could never be like Sasha, chatting away to five people at once—Max had to lip-read to make out what people were saying, and no one at St. Goliath's understood how hard that was. They'd talk quickly, or turn away midsentence, or cover their mouth while they were speaking. Loud classrooms and playgrounds made his hearing aids squeal with feedback, too—after a few minutes, Max would be so exhausted that he had to re-treat to his quiet room with a good book to recover.

Max didn't mind spending time on his own. When he was alone, he could focus on what he was good at: reading voraciously, losing himself in his imagination, designing beautiful models. At school, he always felt like an outsider—like no matter how much everyone tried to include him, he'd never fit in. But on his own, with his latest creation in front of him . . . Max felt like a king.

Then the school had paired him up with Sasha, and Max lost the one place he could escape. It wasn't that Sasha was mean or unpleasant—quite the opposite, in fact. Sasha was super friendly, always asking Max questions and trying to chat—but that was the exact problem. No matter how nice he was, Sasha still didn't understand that Max found talking to people difficult. Being around Sasha was a constant reminder of everything Max struggled to do.

So Max tried to avoid his new roommate as much as possible, ducking out of sight whenever he saw him in the corridors and making sure they were rarely alone. He kept his model-making a secret, too—he suspected that if Sasha found out about it, he'd tell all his friends, and then the whole school would have another reason to treat Max like a complete weirdo.

Sure, it was a bit of a nightmare . . . but it wasn't all bad. Max still had *one* friend at St. Goliath's—Mr. Darrow, the school janitor. If it weren't for their chats and model-making lessons, Max had no idea how he would cope at St. Goliath's. Speaking of which, where *was* . . .

Max stopped. Sasha was leaning in front of his face, waving. Max had explained to Sasha several times that he could just tap him on the shoulder when he wanted Max's attention, but Sasha usually forgot and waved at him like he was flagging down a bus instead.

"Hey! Did you hear me? I *said*, are you doing anything for the holidays?"

Max cringed—he had been hoping no one would ask

him that. He was going to spend eight weeks with his great-aunt Meredith in a retirement community on the other side of the country. She was the only member of his family who was still alive. She was ten times Max's age and could barely remember who he was. She spent most of their time together shouting questions at him until she fell asleep.

"Er . . . nothing much," said Max. "You?"

Sasha grinned. "I'm flying back to the States tonight with my little sister, Joy. First-class all the way! Then Mom and Dad are taking us on a road trip around the country: New York, Texas, San Francisco . . . They said we might even fly to Hawaii for Joy's birthday! Cool, huh?"

Max sighed. Of *course* Sasha had a nice family, too.

They stepped out into the summer sun. The rest of the students were in the distance, watching the headmaster finish his speech. Sasha tapped Max on the shoulder.

"I almost forgot to tell you—Mr. Pitt was talking about the new building! It's going to be amazing—there'll be an Olympic-sized swimming pool, and a new sports hall . . ."

Max nodded, but he wasn't really paying attention—he was trying to spot Mr. Darrow. If he didn't find the janitor soon, then he wouldn't get a chance to show him the model castle before the holidays. He glanced back at Sasha, who was still talking.

". . . and a rooftop planetarium and a sushi kitchen and an augmented-reality science lab . . ."

Max kept one eye on Sasha while searching the playing fields with the other. Maybe Mr. Darrow was in his vegetable patch. That was where he usually went when things at St. Goliath's needed fixing. Max could sneak over there when the speech was over. Then maybe, *finally*, Mr. Darrow would tell him about the secret project, and . . .

". . . Mr. Darrow's disappeared, too. No one knows where he is!"

Max slammed to a halt. Sasha kept on walking.

"Can you believe it? He didn't turn up for work this morning, and when they went to his room, it was empty! He left everything behind—his clothes, his money . . . and you know what else they found? *Models!* Hundreds of them! Turns out he was a complete genius at building things, and no one had any idea!" Sasha shook his head. "Weird, right? I mean, everyone knew he was *odd,* what with all the shouting and swearing, and the fact that he never actually fixed anything, but to disappear without telling anyone? It doesn't make any sense, does it?"

There was silence. Sasha turned round.

"I said, it doesn't make any . . ."

Sasha was alone. Max had left some time ago.

CHAPTER 4

Max stood in the staff corridor. The door in front of him was scuffed and dirty, just like the nameplate.

MR. DARROW

Children weren't supposed to go anywhere near staff bedrooms. It was one of the most important rules at St. Goliath's. You got detention just for setting foot on the top floor of the boardinghouse. Who *knew* what punishment you'd get for breaking into one of the rooms.

But Mr. Darrow had made Max promise.

If one day I suddenly disappear—no warning, no message, no nothing—go straight to my room. Make sure no one sees you . . . especially not Mr. Pitt.

Why?

You'll know when you get there.

Max didn't like breaking rules. It made you stand out—and Max stood out enough already. People were always pointing at his hearing aids, treating him like he was stupid instead of deaf. Mr. Pitt showed him off like a performing seal every time a visitor came to the school.

"This is Max, who, as you can see, has hearing problems. ISN'T THAT RIGHT, MAX? Here at St. Goliath's, we make sure children with disabilities feel just like normal ones. ISN'T THAT RIGHT, MAX?"

Then he'd pat Max on the head, shove him into the wrong classroom, and take the visitors to see the swimming pool.

Max had lost his hearing when he was four years old. He couldn't remember what it was like to *not* be deaf . . . but he could remember his last school. Max had loved it—a little brick building with small classrooms and nice teachers. Max had found it easy making friends there. If he didn't understand something, the teachers would repeat it until he did.

Then two years ago, Great-Aunt Meredith had sent him to St. Goliath's. Suddenly Max was surrounded by hundreds of children in huge classrooms, and teachers who didn't care whether Max understood or not. The only help he ever got was an hour-long visit from a teacher of the deaf who would ask if his hearing aids still worked, barely answer his questions, and then leave. Max never saw the same teacher twice.

But Mr. Darrow was different. He never talked down to Max or treated him like he was a special case—in fact, he was just as rude to Max as he was to everyone else. He might be grumpy, but he was kind too; he took the time to listen. He would explain things as many times as he had to until Max understood.

Why would he have *left*?

Max turned to the framed picture beside the door. It was a watercolor painting of a welcome mat. He carefully reached behind the painting and found the key taped to the wall—just where Mr. Darrow had told him it would be. Max gave one final glance down the corridor, unlocked the door, and stepped inside.

The bedroom was pitch dark. Max reached for the light switch and turned it on. A spray of sparks shot out and scorched his fingers.

"Ow!" said Max.

A bulb flickered weakly. None of the electrics in St. Goliath's worked properly. Boarders had gotten used to the fact that pressing a light switch usually made the bulb explode, or set off all the fire alarms, or resulted in a far-off scream from down a corridor. This was because Mr. Darrow was the worst janitor in history. Instead of doing his job, he was always focused on some unnecessary task, like sorting ten thousand screws into different sizes while the school fell down around him. It was no secret that he and Mr. Pitt despised each other.

Max looked round the bedroom. It was huge, grim and empty. Beside the door was a desk with a heap of old clothes next to it. The floor was covered with hundreds of bits of wire and screws and splinters of wood. On one side of the room was an overturned bin full of old food; on the other side was an unmade bed. There was one window and a broken ceiling fan . . . and that was it. It was pretty depressing, to be honest.

But then, of course, there were the models.

Max's eyes sparkled. He had never seen them all together like this. Mr. Darrow always brought one or two to show him during their model-making lessons, but here . . . there were so many of them. Hundreds. *Thousands,* maybe. And each one was so beautiful, so perfectly constructed, that you would never guess it had been made by human hands.

Max picked up the nearest model. It was a blue whale, no bigger than a goldfish. Its surface was mottled with tiny die-cast barnacles. Each eyeball was an individually carved piece of glass. It was *faultless.* No matter how many times Max studied the model, he always expected it to start breathing.

He remembered the very first time he had seen the whale—the day he met Mr. Darrow. Max could remember that meeting like it was yesterday. It was hard to forget being beaten over the head with a butternut squash.

"Get out my shed!"

Mr. Darrow had chased Max out of the shed, whacking him with the squash.

"I'm sick of you stupid kids! Breaking into my vegetable patch, stealing all my carrots . . . !"

Max wasn't trying to steal Mr. Darrow's carrots. He'd gone wandering round the school to find somewhere quiet to work on his models and stumbled upon Mr. Darrow's potting shed. It was perfect—peaceful and secluded, on the other side of school, where no one would find him. Or so he thought.

"I wasn't stealing anything, I swear!" Max cried. "I was making this!"

Max held up his latest work. It was a model of himself as a brave warrior king, complete with crown and sword, carved into the end of a pencil. Mr. Darrow stopped.

"You made that?"

Max was surprised—he'd expected another whack with the squash, or at the very least to be laughed at . . . but Mr. Darrow was transfixed. He took the model and studied it carefully.

"Mmm—not bad," said Mr. Darrow. "Nice symmetry,

both arms kept a uniform length, good texturing grooves on the robes . . . Face is a mess, though. What you carving with?"

Max held up his old math compass. Mr. Darrow snorted.

"Well, that's your problem right there! Might as well be carving with a brick." He handed the pencil back to Max. "What's your name?"

"Max."

Mr. Darrow reached into his pocket.

"Here, Max—tell me what you think of this one. Finished it yesterday. Like to know your opinion . . . from one model-maker to another."

Mr. Darrow placed the whale in the center of Max's upturned palm. Max stared at the model for some time, almost in shock. He had never seen anything so perfect before.

"I know," said Mr. Darrow, shaking his head. "It's a mess. The inside's even worse."

Max blinked. "There's . . . an inside?"

Mr. Darrow took a set of tweezers from his pocket and opened the whale's mouth. Max was floored. Inside were two precise rows of perfectly sculpted teeth, lined with krill, and a wide speckled tongue draped with seaweed. A bent snorkel no thicker than a human hair stuck out of the roof of the whale's mouth. You could see all the way down its glistening throat. Mr. Darrow pointed with the tweezers.

"See there? Linked the blowhole to the stomach so I could carve the epiglottis. Don't know what I was thinking—they're two completely different organ systems! Ah well."

Max was amazed. "But . . . this is the best model I've ever seen! I'd give *anything* to make something as good as this!"

Mr. Darrow shrugged. "I've been practicing my whole life, Max. Maybe one day—if you never get married or have any children and hate your job—you'll be as good as—"

"Will you teach me?"

The second Max said it, Mr. Darrow's face changed. Max could remember the exact look in the janitor's eyes when it happened. It was like he'd stumbled over the piece of a puzzle he'd lost years ago and then forgotten about.

"Teach you?" Mr. Darrow said, almost to himself.

"I'll practice every day," said Max. "I'm a hard worker."

Mr. Darrow was silent for some time. He chewed thoughtfully on what was left of the squash.

"You know, Max . . . you may be in luck. I could do

with an extra pair of hands. An *apprentice,* if you will. Someone to help me with a big project I've been working on."

"Another model?" said Max.

For the first time, Mr. Darrow had laughed.

"Sort of . . . and sort of not. To tell you the truth, it's more than just a model. It's going to change the world."

Max's eyes widened. "What is it?"

Mr. Darrow shook his head. "I can't tell you—not yet, anyway. First we have to work on that shoddy carving of yours, get you some decent tools. Then, when you're finally good enough, I'll let you in on it. It'll be hard work, you know—don't think I'm going to go easy on you!"

Mr. Darrow had looked at him—and said something no one had said to Max in a very, very long time.

"Did you understand me, Max?"

Max looked around Mr. Darrow's bedroom. He'd *thought* he understood—but he was wrong. He had spent a whole year working with Mr. Darrow, spending every break and lunchtime at his vegetable patch and learning new modeling skills. He'd carved and scraped and sanded until his hands had almost bled. He'd thought they were friends . . . but now Mr. Darrow was gone.

He hadn't even said goodbye.

Max picked up the goggles from the desk beside him. Mr. Darrow had left them too, just like he'd left everything else. It didn't make any sense. The goggles were his most prized possession—he'd let Max wear them only once or twice, and with strict supervision. After all, they were the only ones of their kind in the world.

Just like the models.

That's when Max realized. He looked at the shelves of models, his heart soaring.

"He can't have left! He'd *never* leave the models behind!"

Suddenly it all made sense. Mr. Darrow hadn't disappeared—it was something to do with the secret project. *That* was why he'd told Max to come up here—so he would see the models. So he would understand that Mr. Darrow hadn't abandoned him. He was coming back.

Max looked round the room frantically. He was about to leave for eight whole weeks—he *had* to leave a message for Mr. Darrow, something that showed Max understood. But there wasn't a single pencil or a sheet of paper in sight.

Max took the model castle out of his pocket and grabbed a scalpel from the desk. He quickly carved a series of tiny letters in the base, just above his name:

MR. DARROW
I UNDERSTAND
MAX

Then he walked to the middle of the room and placed the castle on the floor. If Mr. Darrow came back—no, *when* he came back—it would be the first thing he'd see. He'd know straightaway that Max had come up here, just like he'd asked, and . . .

Max stopped. There was something on the floor in front of him, nestled among the screws and splinters and wires. Something so small it was easy to overlook. Max was good at noticing small things—when you've lost your hearing, you rely on your other senses more than most people. People often forgot to get Max's attention before they started talking to him, so he had learned to keep his eyes peeled at all times. He'd see tiny movements, small changes, minute differences. . . .

He'd notice unusual things.

Max picked up Mr. Darrow's microscope goggles and pulled them over his head. The room immediately warped and shifted around him. Max could see every speck of dust. Looking at the back of his hand was like looking at the surface of the moon. He turned to the floor, focused the lenses . . . and frowned.

"What the . . . ?"

Max felt a sudden *bang* through his feet. Most people wouldn't have noticed it—but Max did. A door had been slammed on the floor below. There was another bang, and another.

The speech had finished—everyone was coming back. In a few seconds, the staff corridor was going to be filled with teachers.

Max tore off the goggles and flew out the door. He fumbled for the light switch as he went.

Click.

The light stayed on. Max panicked.

"Come on!"

Click click click.

It was no good—the light wasn't switching off. Max could feel the noises getting stronger and stronger through his feet. He was going to have to leave the room as it was.

Max took one final look at Mr. Darrow's bedroom. There were lots of things he didn't understand—where Mr. Darrow had gone, why he had left . . .

But the thing on the floor made the least sense of all.

Why was there sand in Mr. Darrow's bedroom?

And why was it covered in tiny *palm trees*?

"Weird," said Max.

He closed the door.

CHAPTER 5

Max's footsteps faded down the corridor. The bedroom fell into silence once more.

The light stayed on. It filled the empty room, casting shadows on the models, their glass eyes sparkling.

Of course, the room wasn't *really* empty. There's no such thing as an empty room. There's life wherever you go—mice under the floorboards, moths in the curtains, dust mites in the air . . . there's a whole universe living alongside us and we barely even notice it.

Take the handful of sand on the floor. If Max had studied it for a little longer, he might have seen that it was covered in more than just tiny palm trees. He might have seen that its surface was also flecked with spots of red, green and blue.

He might have seen that the spots were moving.

But Max didn't see the spots tremble and then disappear. He didn't see the sand grow and spread across the floor all by itself. No one did. The world is filled with millions of miracles that no one sees.

No one saw what emerged from the sand, either. It was almost too small to make out . . . and even if someone *had* seen it, they probably wouldn't have believed their eyes.

It was a tiny wooden hut.

8
WEEKS
LATER

CHAPTER 6

The summer holidays were almost over. Mr. Pitt stood at the school gates, practicing his speech.

". . . delighted to welcome you all back to St. Goliath's. . . . As you can see, the Pitt Building is finally complete. . . ."

Not true. The builders had tried to explain to Mr. Pitt that eight weeks wasn't enough time to build everything he'd asked for, but Mr. Pitt was insistent. The school governors were going to arrive at the end of the day, and if they didn't like what they saw, then Mr. Pitt was as good as sacked. He told the builders that if the work wasn't finished on time, they'd be facing a lawsuit so big it'd make their eyes water.

Mr. Pitt wasn't worried—he *always* got what he wanted. Besides, he had a triumphant speech to prepare.

"As headmaster I pride myself on placing students

first . . . care and concern for each one of you, blah blah blah . . ."

He stopped. A boy with a suitcase was walking through the school gates ahead of him.

"Oi, you!" yelled Mr. Pitt. "What are you doing? This is private property!"

The boy stopped in his tracks. "I—I'm Max, sir. I go to school here."

"Never heard of you!" Mr. Pitt barked. "Now get lost, before I shove that suitcase . . ."

The headmaster saw Max's hearing aids and finally remembered who he was. He switched from anger to friendliness like someone changing channels on a TV.

"Ah, Max! How wonderful to— I SAID, HOW WONDERFUL TO SEE YOU."

The shout made Max's hearing aids give a whistle of feedback, and he winced. "You don't need to shout, sir, it actually makes it harder for me to—"

"WHY ARE YOU HERE, MAX? TERM DOESN'T START UNTIL MONDAY."

Max sighed and took a step back so Mr. Pitt couldn't spit on him quite as much.

"My great-aunt Meredith booked my ticket back for today, sir," he explained. "I tried to tell her it was too early, but she just fell asleep. Can I stay in the boarding-house until term starts?"

Mr. Pitt grimaced. "IS THERE NOWHERE ELSE YOU CAN GO?"

Max looked around. "Er . . . I guess I could sleep out here under my suitcase."

Mr. Pitt thought about it.

"THAT'S A KIND OFFER, MAX, BUT SOMEBODY MIGHT SEE YOU." He sighed. "I SUPPOSE YOU'LL HAVE TO STAY IN THE BOARDINGHOUSE."

"Thank you, sir."

"WE'LL BILL YOUR AUNT FOR THE EXTRA DAYS. THIS WAY, PLEASE."

Mr. Pitt grabbed Max's arm and marched him past the building site, trying to block his view.

"NOW, MAX, AS YOU CAN SEE, THE SCHOOL IS MAKING SOME FINAL TWEAKS AND ADJUST-MENTS. NOTHING TO WORRY ABOUT, OF COURSE, BUT I MUST *INSIST* YOU STAY INSIDE THE BOARDINGHOUSE AT ALL TIMES!"

Max grinned. "That's fine by me, sir!"

A weekend in the boardinghouse was exactly what Max wanted. He'd spent the holidays itching to get back to St. Goliath's to see if Mr. Darrow had returned. The janitor would have found Max's castle by now and left him another message. Once Mr. Pitt was gone, Max could sneak upstairs to the staff bedrooms and—

"DON'T WORRY, YOU'LL HAVE PLENTY TO

DO!" said Mr. Pitt. "I'M GOING TO PUT YOU TO WORK WITH THE SUMMER CLUB!"

Max's face fell. "The summer club?"

They came to the boardinghouse, and Max's heart sank. The front doors were covered in streamers and stickers of cartoon unicorns wearing fabulous outfits.

!!*Sparkle Pony Summer Club*!*!*

Max gulped. "Sir—isn't that for five-year-old girls?"

"YES, MAX, FIFTY OF THEM! AND THEY NEED PLENTY OF LOOKING AFTER—UNFORTUNATELY OUR REGULAR STAFF WERE ALL HOSPITALIZED THIS MORNING WHEN ONE OF THEM TOUCHED A LIGHT SWITCH."

Max and Mr. Pitt stepped inside the boardinghouse. Every available surface was coated in glitter glue and sequins. There were three stereos playing three different songs at full volume and fifty girls in fairy wings screaming their heads off.

This was Max's worst nightmare. He could lip-read a conversation with one person if they were facing him and speaking clearly, but adding another person made it twice as hard—it meant Max had to spend the whole time looking back and forth to work out who was talking. Looking after *these* girls would be like playing fifty games of chess blindfolded while someone threw tennis balls at him.

"Sir . . . should I *really* be in charge of all these girls by myself?"

Mr. Pitt looked horrified.

"WHAT—ONE TEN-YEAR-OLD BOY IN CHARGE OF FIFTY YOUNG GIRLS?! OF COURSE NOT! THERE'LL BE TWO OF YOU. . . . AH, THERE HE IS NOW!"

Mr. Pitt pointed to a boy covered from head to toe in screaming girls. It took Max a moment to recognize him.

"*Sasha?*"

Sasha saw Max and turned ghost-white. He looked . . . well, different. He wasn't wearing expensive clothes. In fact, he was wearing a bright-purple unicorn onesie and had a butterfly drawn on his face. He shook off the girls like a dog drying itself.

"M-Max! What are you doing here?!"

Mr. Pitt clapped Sasha on the back, clearly having forgotten the two boys were roommates.

"MAX, THIS IS SASHA! HE'S BEEN HERE ALL SUMMER, HELPING US RUN THE CLUB. THANK-FULLY HE WASN'T ELECTROCUTED WITH THE OTHER TWELVE VOLUNTEERS THIS MORNING. ISN'T THAT RIGHT, SASHA?"

Sasha didn't answer—he was staring at Max like he was going to be sick. He clearly hadn't expected anyone to find him still at school, let alone dressed as a purple unicorn. Mr. Pitt strode toward the door.

"I'LL LEAVE YOU BOYS TO IT! IF YOU NEED ME, I'LL BE UPSTAIRS—I'M GOING TO CHECK MR. DARROW'S ROOM AND MAKE SURE NO ONE'S BROKEN IN!"

Max's heart clenched.

"B-broken in?"

"OH YES!" said Mr. Pitt. "THIS MORNING ONE OF THE BUILDERS NOTICED THE BEDROOM LIGHT HAD BEEN LEFT ON ALL HOLIDAY. A CHILD MUST HAVE SNUCK IN ON THE LAST DAY OF TERM! IF I FIND OUT WHO SET FOOT IN THAT CORRIDOR, I'LL EXPEL HIM SO FAST IT'LL MAKE HIS HEAD SPIN!"

Max's head was spinning already. There could be a message waiting for him in Mr. Darrow's bedroom. And even if there wasn't, Max's model castle was still on the bedroom floor . . . with his name carved into its base.

Several images quickly passed through Max's mind: Mr. Pitt finding the castle; Mr. Pitt expelling Max in front of the whole school; Max spending the rest of his life scraping Great-Aunt Meredith's tongue clean after every meal.

Mr. Pitt stopped at the door to pull out his phone, which had started ringing. Max leapt at the chance.

"J-just going to put my suitcase away, sir!"

Max flew out the door. Mr. Pitt barely noticed him leave, and Sasha was busy trying to scrub the butterfly from his face. Max knew he might have only a few seconds. *Run into Mr. Darrow's room, grab the castle, run out*—that was the plan. If Mr. Pitt caught him before he got back downstairs . . . well, it didn't even bear thinking about.

Max threw his suitcase into a cupboard and sprinted up the stairs to the staff corridor. Sure enough, he could see the light peeking from under Mr. Darrow's bedroom door. He grabbed the key from behind the painting, unlocked the door and threw it open.

As he stepped inside the room, Max was struck by a thought: What if Mr. Darrow *hadn't* come back?

It would mean that no one else had been in the room all summer. It would mean that everything would be exactly as Max had left it. It would mean that behind the door, time would have stood still for eight whole weeks.

After all, thought Max . . . what can happen in an empty room?

THE BOOK OF THE FLOOR

PART 1: THE CREATION OF THE FLOOR

I.   In the beginning—eight weeks ago—there was nothing. The world lay scattered on the Floor and all was in darkness.

II.   Then the Great One opened the Bedroom Door.

III.   He looked upon the darkness and said the word— and the word was Ow.

IV.   And with that, the Bulb came on. The serum in the sand came to life, and it grew and spread until it filled the room from corner to corner, from the Bed unto the Bin.

V.   Then the Great One left again, for some reason.

VI.   But with the light of the Bulb came life, and from the sand came the people of the Floor. They each had hair of different color: some Red, some Green, some Blue. But all were equal, because all were confused.

VII.   They looked upon the Floor and asked, "Where are we?" and "Why are we here?" and many more annoying questions. For truly, no one had the foggiest.

VIII.   Then there came the Wise Man. He was older than time, and knew the answers to all questions.

IX. He gathered the people together, and this is what he said:

X. "Look around you, people of the Floor! THE GREAT ONE has made this place for us!" And the Wise Man explained how the Great One had created the Bulb and the Floor and everything on it.

XI. Then someone asked, "But why would the Great One create us and then leave? That is just bonkers." And all agreed that it was bonkers.

XII. The Wise Man said: "He must protect us from monsters that live beyond the Bedroom Door! They want to destroy our world—and none more so than DEMON!" And the Wise Man explained about Demon, the terrible beast bigger than mountains who hated the people of the Floor and wished them dead—and the people were greatly afraid.

XIII. But the Wise Man said: "Do not fear! The Great One will keep us safe. And one day he will return through the Bedroom Door, and take us all away to Paradise!"

XIV. At this, the people of the Floor were greatly excited; and they cried, "Long live the Great One!"

XV. And someone said, "Wait, sorry, who is this Great One exactly?"

XVI. And the people replied, "Are you serious, Terry, he's the one who created us, try to keep up."

XVII. Then someone asked the Wise Man: "What shall we do with ourselves until the Great One comes back?"

XVIII. The Wise Man gazed upon the Floor, and was silent for some time. He looked at the vast world before him—at the Bulb, and the Bin, and the Bed, and the desert sands that stretched from wall to wall.

XIX. Then he turned to the people—the Reds and the Greens and the Blues—and this is what he said:

XX. "We shall build."

CHAPTER 7

Prince Luke swept the blue hair out of his eyes and faced his kingdom.

Blue Castle shimmered beneath the Bulb light. It was a beautiful sight: the tallest tower stretched over the desert sand, almost three inches in height. The Castle had belonged to the Blues ever since the tribes first scattered across the Floor. Luke's father, King Adam, had discovered it in the desert himself. It just sat there, he said, waiting . . . as if someone had simply left it for them.

Over eight long weeks, the Blues had built huts around the Castle and turned it into a huge city. King Adam had ordered his soldiers to find every splinter of wood on the Floor, and then used those splinters to construct huge walls to protect the city from attacks by the Reds and the Greens. The entire Blue tribe—more than ten thousand people now—lived within the walls.

Luke gulped. In less than a minute, he was going to become their ruler.

"King Luke," he said miserably. "King Luke of the Blues."

He slumped onto the sand. It didn't make any sense. He was about to become one of the most powerful men on the Floor . . . and he was only ten days old.

Luke had never expected to become king. His father had always ruled the Blues. Luke *liked* being a prince. All he had to do was sit around the Castle being waited on by servants and occasionally taking naps. Every now and then somebody would make him go to the library and "study," which as far as Luke could tell meant sitting in front of a table with lots of books on it and falling asleep.

Then, two hours ago, everything changed.

Luke was eating in the grand dining hall. His father was late to dinner, as usual—he was often too busy to eat with the rest of the household. Besides, King Adam was nearly two months old; he needed rest. In fact, Luke thought as he tucked into dessert, his father was resting quite a *lot* nowadays. . . .

Then the dining hall doors burst open, and a dozen Blue soldiers marched into the room. At the front stood Malcolm, the king's advisor. His bright-blue beard, which reached past his knees, was wet with tears.

"The king is . . . dead!" he cried.

The diners gasped in horror. Malcolm held up King Adam's wooden crown and sword.

"He died as he lived . . . throwing things and shouting at his servants!"

The dining hall was in uproar. King Adam—*dead?* He had always ruled the Blues—without him in charge, the tribe would have starved to death weeks ago! Who could possibly replace him?

Luke was asking himself that exact question when Malcolm turned to him with the crown.

"Arise, King Luke!"

It was that simple: one moment Luke was on his second helping of jelly, the next moment everyone was bowing down to him. He nearly choked.

"Me? *King?!*"

"Yes, you!" said Malcolm. "Now come on—*arise!*"

Luke didn't know what *arise* meant, so he stood up instead. Malcolm started lowering the crown onto his head.

"That looks heavy," Luke whimpered.

"For Great One's sake, Luke—try to look like a king," Malcolm whispered. "Everyone's watching!"

Malcolm put the crown on Luke's head. Luke's legs buckled under the weight, and he hit the floor like a rail of shirts.

After that, everyone agreed that they should do a

"proper" coronation—one where Luke didn't fall over. All ten thousand Blues would gather below the tallest tower to watch him take up his father's sword, recite the entire Book of the Floor by heart, and become their new king.

The only problem was Luke didn't *want* to become king. He wasn't anything like his father: he was clumsy and forgetful and small for his age. He had no idea how to lead an army, or give speeches, or defend the city from attacks by the Reds and the Greens. Now he'd be responsible for ten thousand Blues, all of whom needed feeding, and the only way to do that was to make the long quest to the Bin Kingdom. The leader of the Green tribe, the Bin King, had claimed the Bin when the tribes first scattered, and now it was the only source of food on the Floor. The Bin King could force the other tribes to pay ransom whenever he felt like it, and he usually did. Luke would have to make the perilous journey across the Floor to negotiate prices, then transport all the food back to Blue Castle while avoiding bands of Red marauders. He had never even been outside the city walls before.

Second by second, the coronation grew closer.

The final rehearsal for the coronation had been a complete disaster. During the bit where Luke was supposed to take up his father's sword and swear to protect the kingdom, he'd tripped over his robes, which were far too big for him, and sliced off Malcolm's beard.

"For Great One's sake!" cried Malcolm, tying his beard back on. "The ceremony is only a few minutes away, and you're *still* not ready! *Please* tell me you've at least learned the Book of the Floor by now. . . ."

Luke cringed.

"I've been trying, honest! There's just so *much*. . . . I know the first bit, where the Great One makes everything and the Wise Man appears, but after that . . ."

Malcolm was furious. He shoved the Book into Luke's hands.

"Go out into the desert," he snapped, "and don't come back till you've learned it!"

Luke was on the verge of tears. "Malcolm, please— I don't know how to do this! I'm not my father!"

But Malcolm wasn't listening. Luke made his way miserably to the stables and found his prized flea, Excelsior. She was one of the finest steeds on the Floor: sleek, polished and intelligent. Luke had found her when she was just a pupa and raised her himself. She was his best and only friend.

Excelsior squeaked happily when she saw him and hopped in circles, trying to play with him.

"Not now, girl," said Luke glumly. "We've got work to do."

Luke jumped on her back and she bounded out from the city walls. They rode until Blue Castle was far behind them and there was nothing around but desert. Luke climbed off Excelsior and patted her side affectionately.

"Off you go, girl. Not too far now."

Excelsior hopped across the dunes, leaving Luke by himself. He sighed. There was a time when the thought of being outside the city on his own would have terrified him, but Red marauders and sand spiders didn't frighten him anymore. There were much scarier things waiting for him back at Blue Castle.

Luke took off his father's crown and sword and threw them to one side. He wished he felt sadder about his father's death, but the truth was Luke had barely known him. King Adam might have been a great ruler, but he was a rubbish dad. The only quality time they ever spent together was once a day, on Luke's Birth-Minute, when King Adam would storm into his bedroom, ask Luke why he was still so small, then storm out again. Whenever Luke tried to ask about his mother, whom he had never known, or tried to tell King Adam that he was bored inside the Castle with no one to play with except his pet flea, his father simply hadn't listened.

"I guess the only one who really listens to me is *you*, Excelsior."

But Excelsior wasn't paying attention—she was busy digging in the sand for crumbs. Luke grumbled and opened the Book of the Floor instead.

"*. . . So the Wise Man sent the people across the Floor to explore and build their world. . . . And so it was that the tribes settled into their respective kingdoms: the Reds at the Bed, the Greens in the Bin, and the Blues in the Castle . . . and there they waited for the moment when the Great One would return through the Bedroom Door. . . .*"

Luke gazed up at the Bedroom Door. It dominated the wall ahead of him, stretching up higher than he could make out. He couldn't imagine how something could simply walk through it—it was like trying to imagine the sky falling, or the Bulb going out. But supposedly, one day, that was exactly what would happen. The Great One would come back to the Floor and take them away. Because he loved them. Because he wanted to protect them.

Because he was always listening.

"Are you there?"

Luke's voice faded across the dunes. He swallowed.

"Great One, I know you're busy fighting Demon and

47

everything, but if you *are* listening, then please ... help me."

The Bedroom Door stood still and silent. The only sound was Excelsior chasing her own antenna in the distance.

"I'm not ready for this," said Luke. "I can't protect the city from the Reds, or stop the Bin King from raising food prices. . . . I'm too young to be king!"

He let his words drift over the desert.

"Please—find someone else to do it. Stop the coronation. Just do ... *something.*"

Luke waited expectantly. The desert was silent.

Nothing.

Luke let out a deep sigh. Of *course* nothing happened. The Great One wasn't listening to him really. Luke was just another tiny voice. He turned to Blue Castle, waiting for him in the distance.

"Oh well," he said. "Here goes noth—"

The world turned black.

Luke gasped. A great wave of darkness spread across the dunes, blackening the sand and heading toward his kingdom. Luke watched as the enormous shadow stole across the rooftops and swallowed the Castle in darkness.

Excelsior bounded back to him, burying her head in his armpit and squeaking in terror. Luke stood bolted to the spot, his heart pounding. He had seen some-thing like this before, when he was three days old. A fly had flown in front of the Bulb and cast its shadow on the Floor. Luke had been terrified—he thought it was a huge monster creeping over the sand to eat him. He thought it was *Demon*.

But this was no fly. This was *huge*. There was noth-ing on the Floor that was this big.

Nothing except—

Luke turned around, and his mouth fell open in amazement.

The Bedroom Door was opening, right in front of his eyes. A vast rectangle of shadow was cutting across the Bulb, splitting the Floor in two.

And standing in the Doorway was . . .

CHAPTER 8

Max opened the door and stepped inside.

He was speechless.

The first thing he noticed was that Mr. Darrow's bedroom had changed. Lots of things were the same: the bulb was still on, the bed was still unmade . . .

But the entire floor was covered in sand.

It didn't make any sense. When Max had left, there'd only been a handful of sand beside the castle, but that was . . .

Max stopped. He had just seen the castle.

There was a flag sticking out of the top of it.

The flag was tiny—no bigger than a stamp. That wasn't the only thing that was different about the castle. It also had wooden walls around it, with gates and guard posts and watchtowers.

And *inside* the walls were . . .

Max grabbed the microscope goggles from Mr. Darrow's desk and marched over to the castle. He crouched down, pulled the goggles over his head and focused on the floor beneath him. His breath caught in his throat.

The castle was surrounded by hundreds of miniature wooden huts. *Thousands,* in fact. The huts had doorways and windows and roofs made of microscopic palm leaves, and chimneys with actual smoke coming out of them. Max could even see furniture and fireplaces and unmade beds through their minuscule hand-carved windows.

And standing in the streets, staring up at him, were thousands upon thousands of tiny blue-haired people.

Max laughed in disbelief. The people were no bigger than ants, and there was every kind of person you could imagine: young people and old people and dukes and duchesses and babies and beggars, all staring back up at him. They were so realistic that Max could *swear* some of them were actually pointing at him too.

Mr. Darrow hadn't just come back—he'd turned Max's castle into a *kingdom.* It was the most beautiful, perfect, intricate model Max had seen in his entire life. Who else but Mr. Darrow could have made it? Who else could have created an entire city filled with thousands of handmade people, who really did look like they were pointing up at Max and screaming and running away and . . .

Max stopped. He took the goggles off, blinked a few times and looked back down. This time, he really *couldn't* believe his eyes.

He wasn't imagining it. This wasn't like the time he accidentally inhaled too many model glue fumes and thought his bedroom ceiling was made of toast. The tiny people *were* running away from him. All of them.

It all happened in the blink of an eye, like watching a sped-up film. The people scattered through the city at superfast speed, making whisper-quiet squeaks of terror. Max could see parents pulling their children into huts and slamming the doors, and soldiers leaping onto the backs of fleas and riding away, and crowds pouring down side streets like trickles of bright-blue rainwater . . .

This wasn't a model. These weren't handmade people. They were *alive*.

And then Max saw a tiny movement on the sand in front of him.

It was a boy. He was standing on his own outside the city, just in front of Max's right foot. If Max had moved another centimeter forward, he'd have crushed the boy like a bug without realizing it.

Max stared at the boy. The boy stared back. He had bright-blue hair, and bright-blue eyes, and bright-blue robes that were far too big for him.

And balanced on his head was a tiny wooden crown.

CHAPTER 9

Luke stared at the giant, and the giant stared back.

It had cleared the desert between the Doorway and Blue Castle in five enormous strides, each footstep shuddering through the sand like an earthquake. It moved with unbelievable slowness—Luke should have taken the chance to run, but he couldn't. He had stayed frozen to the spot, right until the giant had slammed an enormous white trainer onto the sand directly in front of him. Excelsior had given a terrified squeak and instantly fled.

"Excelsior, you coward! Come back here!"

But it was no use—Luke was alone with the giant. He had watched in speechless terror as it leaned toward him like a mountain falling to earth, until it was so close that Luke could feel its breath pounding on the sand like a hurricane....

And then he had seen its face.

Luke knew at once that it wasn't the Great One. It was a *monster*. Luke had never seen anything so terrifying before. It had eyes that stuck out of its head on great glass stalks, and vast machines where its ears should be. Behind him, he could hear thousands of screams from Blue Castle. His people were terrified too—they needed protecting.

They needed a king.

"Oh crud," Luke whimpered.

He reached down and picked up the crown and the sword with shaking hands. He could already hear his father's voice inside his head.

Luke, what are you doing?

I'm going to kill the giant.

That's the stupidest thing I've ever heard.

I have to. I'm king.

Not yet, actually.

Shut up.

Luke gripped the sword with both hands, took a deep breath . . . and looked up.

He was shocked by what he saw. The giant had changed. Its long stalk eyes were gone—in fact, its eyes were now just like Luke's.

The giant didn't look scary anymore. It was even smiling at him. It looked . . . well, *he* looked nice.

Luke was stuck. Was he still supposed to kill the

giant, even if the giant was smiling? That didn't seem very friendly. But what if the giant changed again? What if he suddenly crushed the kingdom with one hand and swallowed Luke whole? What if—

Luke stopped. The giant was opening his mouth.

Like everything the giant did, it happened slowly— millimeter by millimeter. Luke saw the lips part, and the teeth separate, and the back of its throat flicker into life. . . .

And then the sound came.

It was like planets crashing into each other. Volcanoes erupting. It blasted against Luke like an explosion, pounding across the desert like the end of the world, until Luke was running away as fast as he could.

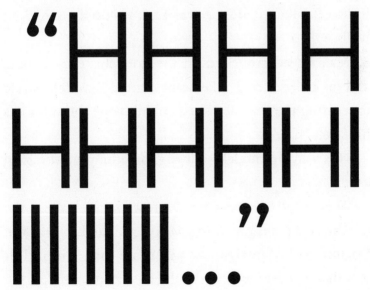

"HHHH HHHHHI ||||||||||. . ."

CHAPTER 10

"Hi," said Max.

It felt like a stupid thing to say, but Max had never spoken to a tiny king before. He thought being friendly was a good start.

Nope. The boy shot across the sand like a gunshot. In less than a second, he was back inside the kingdom walls.

Max stayed crouched on the floor, his eyes shining and his pulse racing. Maybe he should have felt worse for scaring the boy—but he couldn't wipe the smile off his face.

"It's a living model—a living, breathing model *kingdom!*"

This was it—*this* was Mr. Darrow's secret project, the one he had been preparing Max for all along. And Mr. Darrow had been right—it *was* more than a model. It was the greatest invention in the history of mankind.

Max was so excited that it took him a while to realize someone behind him was tapping him on the shoulder.

He spun round. Standing behind him, still wearing the unicorn onesie, was Sasha.

Max's stomach dropped. He suddenly remembered where he was, and what he was supposed to be doing. He leapt to his feet, trying to block the castle from view.

"S-Sasha! What are you doing here?"

"Er . . . I came to find you," said Sasha. "Mr. Pitt got a call from the builders and had to leave. Apparently the revolving dance floor in the new staff room isn't working."

Max nodded, sweat breaking out across his forehead. He had to get Sasha away from here. If his roommate caught so much as a glimpse of the tiny kingdom, Mr. Darrow's creation would be discovered and it would all be over. Max strode toward the door.

"I see! Well, let's get back downstairs before—"

He made it halfway to the door before Sasha grabbed him.

"Don't tell anyone! Please!"

Max was completely thrown. "Huh?"

"Everyone thinks I'm back in the States!" Sasha cried. "If they find out I've been here the whole time, running the Sparkle Pony Summer Club . . . Don't you get it, Max? I'll be the laughingstock of the whole school!"

"Sasha, calm down. . . ."

But Sasha wouldn't calm down—and he wouldn't move either. Max kept trying to push him out the door, but it was no use.

"Sasha, come on—I'm not going to tell anyone!"

Sasha was shocked. "You're not?"

"Of course not! If you don't want me to say anything, I won't! Now—let's—*go!*"

Max kept trying to bundle Sasha out the door, but it was like trying to fight a golden retriever. Now Sasha was beaming from ear to ear and shaking Max's hand.

"Max, thank you! I knew you were a good guy! What can I do to repay you?"

"You can get out the door!" Max shoved harder. "Quick, before—"

"Is that a castle?"

Max froze.

"Er . . . pardon?"

Sasha was staring over Max's shoulder.

"There's . . . there's a little castle. On the floor, behind you."

Max had to come up with a lie, quick. "Yes! It is! A model castle! Mr. Darrow made models, remember? Now let's—"

"Max?"

"Yes?"

"It's, er . . . moving."

Max almost couldn't bring himself to look, but he knew he had to.

The walls of the kingdom were covered in hundreds of tiny knights. They were all wearing wooden armor and clambering up the watchtowers at superfast speed, filling the guard posts and gateways. They stood in position, facing Max and Sasha with spears no bigger than splinters . . . and uttered a tiny, furious battle squeak.

There was a long pause.

"Max?"

"Yes?"

"Are those people *alive*?"

Max gulped. He knew what he had to do now. If he wanted to protect Mr. Darrow's creation, then he was going to have to blackmail Sasha. He was going to have to say that if Sasha didn't keep quiet, then Max would make sure everyone in school knew about the Sparkle Pony Summer Club. There was no *way* that Sasha would understand how important this was, how precious and unique and—

"That's *incredible!*"

Max stopped midthought. Sasha was staring at the kingdom in complete amazement, his mouth hanging open.

"Can you believe it? It's a living, breathing model *kingdom*! With little knights and everything! It's like something out of *Dragon Rider*!"

Max blinked. "You've read *Dragon Rider*?"

Sasha shrugged. "Er . . . well, I read your copy when you weren't in the room. I thought you wouldn't mind." He turned back to the castle. "But this . . . this is for real! Look at it! It must be the most incredible invention in the history of the world!"

Suddenly Sasha didn't look like the coolest boy in school. He looked like—well, he looked even more excited than Max felt. Max had always thought they had nothing in common, nothing to talk about. But it looked like he'd been wrong.

"What's it *doing* here?"

Max had always preferred working on models to talking with people. Models were easy to understand. They stayed the same—at least, they *usually* did. People talked too fast, and changed their minds without warning, and veered off on different subjects just as Max was able to grasp what they were talking about. With models, you always knew where you were. They never surprised you.

But sometimes, Max realized, being surprised by someone was really nice.

"Sasha," he said, "can you keep a secret?"

CHAPTER 11

Luke ran through the city gates, gasping for breath.

He could barely think—the giant's bellow had rattled his brains to thought-paste. The shout had the same effect on the rest of the kingdom. Every hut door was shut; every family peeked out their windows while clutching their loved ones close. Only soldiers were in the streets, and they looked as frightened as Luke did.

"*Your Majesty!*"

Malcolm was racing toward him, flanked by a dozen soldiers.

"Thank the Great One you're alive! We've been looking for you everywhere—we thought they'd got you!"

Luke frowned. "*They?* What do you—"

Luke stopped dead. There was *another* giant in the Doorway now, standing behind the first one. But this second giant was different—bright purple, with a huge spike sticking out of its head. It was also taller, and cooler, and had a better haircut.

"Malcolm," Luke whispered, "what *are* those things?"

Malcolm shuddered with fear.

"Monsters from beyond the Bedroom Door—the ones the Wise Man warned us about! They must have found a way inside! Now there is nothing to protect us from the might of . . . *Demon!*"

Malcolm pointed to the first of the two giants with a trembling hand. Luke was confused—the giant still didn't look like a monster to him. Sure, it had bellowed into his face like a bomb going off, but that was it. Apart from that, it seemed . . . well, friendly.

"Malcolm, are you *sure* that's Demon?"

"There's no time for questions, Your Majesty!" Malcolm grabbed Luke's arm. "The kingdom is under attack! We have to get you out of here!"

A plain black carriage pulled up beside them. Six fleas were harnessed to the front, bucking against their reins and screeching in fear.

"I'm sending you to a secret hideout on the other side of the Floor, with your two best guards," Malcolm said breathlessly. "Your father used it many times when traveling in the desert. Stay hidden and stay safe,

Luke—your people need their leader! I'll come to find you when this is all over!"

Luke gawped. "The desert? But I can't..."

Malcolm wasn't listening. He tied a cape round Luke's shoulders.

"We all have one moment in our life that matters, Your Majesty. One single moment. You must save yourself for when it's your time, and make that moment count."

"*Look out!*"

Soldiers were pouring from every corner of the city, their sights fixed on the two giants in the Doorway. The giants stood side by side, gazing down at the kingdom. They were looking right at Luke.

And they were—

"*They've seen the prince!*" screamed Malcolm. "*Get him out of here!*"

Two burly guards shoved Luke into the carriage and jumped in, one on either side of him. With that, the fleas sped out of the city walls and away from the Door. The kingdom disappeared, and soon there was nothing but desert as far as the eye could see.

Luke sat wedged between the guards, his mind reeling. He had asked for something—*anything*—to stop the coronation, and he had gotten exactly what he wished for. Who knew what was going to happen now? Why were the giants here? What did they *want*?

But all Luke could think about was what he had seen the giants doing.

They'd been looking at him. They'd been holding up their hands and moving them very, *very* slowly from side to side.

Had they been *waving* at him?

CHAPTER 12

Max and Sasha waved at the tiny king. They watched as he was bundled into a carriage and carried to the other side of the room in a flash.

"Wow!" said Sasha. "They're *fast*."

Max nodded. "They must live at a higher speed than we do."

The two boys looked at the kingdom in silence. The knights still manned the walls, and the ten thousand other blue-haired people continued to cower inside their huts. Every now and then, one of them would peek out, give an almost inaudible squeak of terror and slam the hut door again. Sasha rubbed his head.

"So . . . let me get this straight. Mr. Darrow *made* this?"

Max nodded. "The sand, the huts, the walls around the castle: none of it was here last term. The people weren't, either."

65

Sasha was amazed. "Mr. Darrow made *them,* too?"

Max nodded. Sasha opened and closed his mouth a few times before sound came out.

"How?"

Max held up his hands hopelessly. "I haven't got a clue! He never told me what he was making, just that he'd need my help when it was ready. He must have been sneaking back in here over the holidays to build it!"

"Back from where?"

Max sighed. "I don't know *that,* either. He used to take these weird holidays sometimes. He'd tell Mr. Pitt that he was ill and needed a few days off, but he was secretly traveling all over the world. He never told me where he was going, just that he was looking for something important. Something for the project. Maybe he finally found something to make the model come to life—and now he has to keep going back there to get more!"

Max gazed down at the tiny kingdom.

"Which means that until Mr. Darrow gets back, this is my responsibility. I have to make sure Mr. Pitt doesn't find out about it."

Sasha frowned. "Why?"

"Pitt *hates* Mr. Darrow!" said Max. "If he comes up here and finds the castle, then he'll make sure Mr. Darrow never sees it again. He'll probably even try to get Mr. Darrow arrested for breaking back into the school."

Max shook his head. "I can't let that happen. I can't let Mr. Darrow down after everything he's done for me."

"So what are we going to do?" said Sasha.

Max sighed. "I do have *one* idea, but—"

He stopped midsentence.

"Hang on . . . did you say *we*?"

Sasha nodded. "Of course! I'm going to help you!"

Max was dumbstruck. "But, Sasha, Mr. Pitt said he'd expel anyone who set foot in the staff corridor, remember? If he finds out you're involved—"

Sasha put a hand on Max's shoulder and cut him off. "Max, you said you wouldn't tell anyone about the Sparkle Pony Summer Club. That's the first nice thing anyone's done for me since I moved here. Friends help each other out—and when I make friends with someone, I mean it."

Max was stunned. "We're friends?"

"Sure we are!" said Sasha. "I mean, we both like the same things, we're both ten . . . besides, we're roommates, aren't we? If that doesn't make us friends, then I don't know what does!"

He took Max's index finger and crossed his own over it, like the fingers were hugging.

"*Friends!*"

Max was shocked. Deep down, he had always thought Sasha was only being nice to him to be kind. People at school did that all the time. They'd start off asking Max questions and including him in their conversations, but when Max couldn't keep up, they'd stop trying and leave him behind.

But it looked like Max had had Sasha all wrong. Sasha wasn't like everyone else. Sasha was . . . well, he was really nice.

"Er . . . OK, then," said Max. "Friends."

Sasha gave him a huge smile, then let go of Max's finger and clapped the air. Max jumped.

"What was that?"

"Sorry!" said Sasha. "Just a fly. Got it, though."

He wiped his hand on his onesie and patted Max on the back.

"So, Max—tell me about this plan of yours."

CHAPTER 13

Max and Sasha stood in front of the Sparkle Pony Summer Club.

"So that's the plan," said Sasha. "Max and I have to leave you alone for a bit, and until we get back, *no one* leaves this room! Understand? Not to go to the kitchen, not to go to the toilet and *especially* not to go outside!"

"But, *Saaaaaaashaaaaaa.*"

A girl shoved her way to the front of the crowd. She looked and sounded exactly like Sasha—she was even wearing an identical purple unicorn onesie. The only differences were that she was half Sasha's height, had her hair in pigtails and wore an enormous badge on the front of her onesie that said 5 TODAY.

"You said we were going to spend the day with me!"

Sasha looked guilty. "Joy, I know I did, but I'll only be gone a little while. . . ."

Joy stared at her brother for a moment. Then, very

slowly, her mouth began to open. No sound came out at first—her mouth just kept getting wider and wider, until it took up most of her face. It was like watching a solar eclipse.

Then the sound arrived.

"AAAAAAAAAAAAAAAAAAAAAAAAAAAAAA . . ."

Max's hearing aids gave an almighty wail of feedback. Sasha didn't even blink.

"Joy, stop it."

"AAAAAAAAAAAAAAAAAAAAAAAAAAAAAA . . ."

"I said stop—"

"AAAAAAAAAAAAAAAAAAAAAAAAAAAAAA . . ."

"Come on, it's only for a few minutes!"

Joy stopped crying. "You *promised* you'd spend the whole day with me, remember? You said you'd make my birthday *perfect* because Mom and Dad can't . . . can't . . ."

Joy couldn't go on. Her face crumpled and she burst into tears. Sasha knelt and hugged her close.

"Hey, hey, hey, come on, shhh. . . . Look, I'm sorry, I'm just a silly older brother. Come on, stop crying."

Tears turned to sniffles. Sasha wiped Joy's eyes.

"I'll only be a few minutes, that's all. I can't tell you why, but it's super important. When I get back we'll do dance routines, make cakes—"

"Can I give you a makeover?" said Joy.

"Not in a million years. But I'll put on *The Sparkle Pony Movie*. How about that?"

All the girls gasped. The air pressure in the room dropped considerably.

"How many times?" said Joy.

"Once."

"It's my birthday. Twice."

"*Once*, Joy."

"Once, but you sing along with all the songs."

Sasha rolled his eyes. "Fine."

The girls lifted Joy onto their shoulders and ran round the room screaming with triumph. Sasha watched with a big proud smile on his face.

"My little sister! Isn't she cute?"

"Sure," said Max.

The two boys crept outside and sidestepped round the boardinghouse like spies, checking for any sign of Mr. Pitt. When the coast was clear, they dashed into the bushes.

"You're good at that, you know," said Max.

Sasha looked at him. "Good at what?"

"Taking care of those girls."

Sasha snorted. "You learn fast when you have Joy for a sister! I guess she's more delicate than usual today, seeing as it's her birthday and we're not with Mom and Dad. She nearly screamed her head off this morning when I said I didn't want to wear the same onesie as her."

They pushed through the bushes.

"So . . . why *aren't* you with your parents?" asked Max.

Sasha blushed. "The family trip got canceled at the last second. Mom and Dad both work hard—we've moved around a lot the last few years. That's why they sent us to this boarding school. They usually get the summer off to make up for being so busy all the time, but they had some kind of 'work emergency' and Joy and I had to stay here."

Max was shocked. "Sasha, that's terrible."

Sasha shrugged. "It's not so bad. The girls are nice enough—you just have to make sure they don't have too much sugar or they go crazy. I had to take away all their candy on the first day and hide it in our dorm. You should have heard them *scream*."

Max was confused. "But . . . I don't get it. Why didn't you just stay with one of your friends instead?"

Sasha laughed. "Like who?"

Max thought about it. "Well, like *any* of those people you hang around with. You're the most popular boy in school!"

Sasha shook his head. "None of those people are my friends, Max—not *real* friends, anyway. I talk to them, but that's it. Why do you think I've been trying to talk to you all year?"

Max was amazed. He'd always thought he was good at noticing things, but somehow he'd gotten Sasha all wrong.

"It was different when I was back in the States," sighed Sasha. "I had tons of friends there—I miss them like crazy. People here are nice, but no one actually wants to get to know me. I'm just 'the American kid.' Do you ever get that feeling sometimes, like you're on show? Like no matter how much people try to include you, you'll never actually fit in?"

Max stared at him.

"Yeah," he said. "Yeah, I do."

There was a moment of quiet. Sasha pointed over Max's shoulder.

"Is that it? Mr. Darrow's vegetable patch?"

Max peered from between the bushes—sure enough, they had arrived. The garden was like a lush jungle paradise, filled with every vegetable you could possibly think of. Plants sprouted from deep beds on every side, separated into perfect rectangles with signs saying GET OUT and GO AWAY and IF I CATCH YOU STEALING MY CARROTS AGAIN I'M GOING TO CUT YOUR THUMBS OFF.

"People steal his carrots?" said Sasha.

"Don't ask," said Max.

The boys made their way to a wooden shed and threw open the door. Inside, it was dry and sun-warmed and dusty. Tables piled high with dirty gloves and plant pots ran along the walls.

"This is where Mr. Darrow keeps all his tools," Max explained. "We'll need a spade—something large enough to scoop up the castle and all the people in one go. We can put them into one of these big seedling trays, carry it downstairs and keep them safe in our dorm until Mr. Darrow gets back!"

Sasha gave him a thumbs-up. "Great! You look for the shovel, I'll find a tray!"

The boys set to work.

"So," said Sasha, "you and Mr. Darrow are really friends?"

Max nodded. "We used to model together every day. Sometimes at break *and* lunchtime."

Sasha laughed. "No wonder I could never find you!"

Max blushed. "Yeah, well, Mr. Darrow's very serious about making models. He's probably the best modeler in the world."

"Then how come he's so terrible at fixing things?"

"He's not terrible!" said Max. "He just . . . gets distracted."

"*Distracted?*" said Sasha. "The swimming pool's been broken since I got here."

"That's not Mr. Darrow's fault!" said Max. "He took out the filter, then decided to make all the new parts himself, and—"

"There's not a single light switch in school that works properly."

Max looked uncomfortable. "Yeah, well, he had to organize all those bits of wire into different lengths first—"

"It took him a week to put out that fire."

Max sighed. "Here, look at this."

He pulled out one of his hearing aids, which gave a whistle of feedback. There was a small rubber mold that fit inside the ear, and a thin tube that led to a plastic case that fit round the back. Inside the case were a tiny microphone, an amplifier and a battery pack. The case was covered in tiny fault lines, like the cracks in a snowflake.

"See those cracks? That's where it's been glued back together. It fell out in phys ed last year and someone stepped on it by accident. I was going to have to send it away to be repaired, which normally takes *weeks*. I would've only been able to hear from one side until it came back, too—and it's hard enough for me to follow what's going on as it is." Max smiled. "I showed it to Mr. Darrow, and he fixed it in one day. He made it ten times better, too. I can hear things I've never been able to before. And look!"

Max pointed to a tiny button in the middle of the

battery pack, no bigger than the head of a pin. It had a microscopic X chiseled above it. Max pressed the button, and a tinny sound came out.

"Sport radio!" said Max. "Mr. Darrow installed it as a surprise—now I can listen to football in class without anyone knowing!"

Sasha frowned. "Do you *like* football?"

"Er . . . no," said Max. "But it's better than nothing."

Max put the hearing aid back in, and it gave another screech of feedback as he did. Sasha grimaced.

"*Yowch*. Does it always make that sound?"

Max nodded. "When I put it in and take it out. And if it's loose. With loud noises, too."

Sasha shook his head. "I had no idea."

Max smiled. "It's fine. Most people don't."

Max usually hated it when people asked about his hearing aids—sometimes they'd ask before even saying hello. But Max didn't mind when Sasha did it—in fact, it felt good to talk about it. He grabbed a shovel.

"Well, this should do the trick! Got a tray?"

Sasha held one up. "Let's go!"

They raced back to the boardinghouse, glancing round every corner to make sure Mr. Pitt was nowhere near. By the time they reached Mr. Darrow's door, they were panting and covered in sweat.

"We'd better be quick," said Max. "Mr. Pitt could be back any moment!"

Sasha looked nervous. "You sure we're not too late already? We've been gone a while. . . ."

Max started unlocking the door.

"It'll be fine. I mean, how much could have happened in twenty minutes?"

CHAPTER 14

Luke stood in the desert, staring at the smoking ruins.

"My . . . my kingdom."

There was nothing left of Blue Castle. The city walls had been torn down. The huts had been torched. His people were nowhere to be seen.

A lot had happened in the past twenty minutes.

Twenty minutes earlier, Luke had arrived at the hideout, a tiny hut without windows on the edge of the desert. The guards had ushered Luke inside, then stood in front of the door and refused to budge.

"How long are we here for?" Luke asked. "When are we going back?"

Silence.

"I command you to answer me!" said Luke. "I am your king! Almost."

Nothing. So Luke had sat and listened to the sounds of the desert. There were lots of them: the booming footfalls of the giants as they walked across the Floor, the thunderclap of their voices as they spoke to one another . . .

After a while, there was another sound, one Luke had never heard before. A low, buzzing drone that seemed to fill the entire sky.

Then came another sound, right outside the hut. Footsteps. Voices. Swords being drawn.

"What *is* that?" he'd asked the guards.

Without a word, the guards had flown out of the hut. Before he knew what was happening Luke heard yells and clashes, terrible shrieks of pain, bodies hitting the hut walls . . .

And then, silence.

Luke had waited for what felt like an eternity. When he couldn't bear the silence any longer—and when it became obvious that the guards were not coming back—he crept to the door and peeked out-side.

The desert was empty, stretching out as silent as a cemetery. The giants were nowhere to be seen, and the Bedroom Door was shut.

Luke's guards lay dead on the sand.

Next to them lay the bodies of eight other soldiers.

They weren't Blue soldiers. Their armor was made of tinfoil, and their swords were giant toothbrush bristles sharpened to points.

They all had green hair.

Luke's heart raced. Green soldiers had come to kill him. He had to get back home, right away. On the horizon was a thin trail of smoke: it *had* to be coming from Blue Castle. Grabbing his crown and sword, he set off across the sand.

And now Luke stood in front of the smoldering remains of his kingdom.

He wandered through the empty streets like a ghost, gazing at the devastation. The only thing left standing was the castle itself, and even that was gouged and battered by catapult fire. No sign of life anywhere, except...

"Excelsior!"

His flea was burrowing through a heap of scorched wood. She was filthy and disheveled, but she squeaked with joy when she saw Luke and hopped over, snuffling his face.

"Oh, girl, what *happened* here? Where did everybody—"

Luke stopped. Right in front of him were the broken castle gates. All the statues of his father had been toppled and smashed to pieces.

Written above the archway in bright-green paint were the words:

THE AGE OF THE GREEN FLOOR HAS BEGUN

"Your Highness!"

Luke looked up. Hanging from the flagpole on top of the tallest tower was a cage. Malcolm was chained inside it.

"Wait right there!" cried Luke. "I'm coming!"

Luke dashed up the spiral staircase as fast as he could. It was the exact journey he would have made on the way to his coronation, but that seemed like a lifetime away now. He reached the top of the tower and winched down the cage.

Malcolm was a sorry sight—he had been left with only his underpants and his beard to cover him—but Luke had never been so happy to see another person in his life. They embraced through the bars, tears streaming down their faces.

"Oh, Your Highness!" Malcolm cried. "I thought they'd got you, too! I . . . I . . ."

"Malcolm, what *happened*?" asked Luke. "The kingdom—my people—*the Green Floor* . . . What is . . . ?"

Luke trailed off. What he had seen over Malcolm's shoulder was enough to chill his blood.

On the far horizon of the desert was a huge cylinder, with an opening at its front like a vast black moon. Inside was pure darkness. It was the Bin, the kingdom of the Green tribe.

And flying in and out of the Bin were . . .

"Malcolm," Luke whispered, "what *is* that?"

Malcolm didn't reply at first. When Luke turned back, he was shocked to see that his father's advisor—the oldest and most sensible man Luke knew—looked even more frightened than Luke felt.

"*That*, Your Highness," he said, "is war."

CHAPTER 15

Max and Sasha stood in the doorway in silence.

Mr. Darrow's bedroom was filled with flies. Not just one or two, but hundreds of them. They buzzed around the room in every direction, hovering a few centimeters above the floor.

And that wasn't even the worst of it.

"The castle!" Max cried.

It was in ruins. A single thread of smoke curled through the air above it. The blue-haired people were nowhere to be seen.

"They're—they're gone! What happened? Where could they possibly—"

Sasha pointed across the room. "There!"

Sure enough, on the other side of the room was a crowd of blue people scuttling across the sand like superfast bugs.

Sasha shook his head. "Why are they over *there*?"

Max frowned. "They're heading toward that bin in the corner! See? The one on its side, with all the flies coming out of it and—"

Max stopped. He had just seen what was inside the bin.

He hadn't bothered looking at the bin earlier. All his attention had been focused on the castle.

Now he could see that it *wasn't* just a bin.

Inside the bin was a city of tiny buildings and factories and houses made out of rubbish. There were matchbox skyscrapers and drinks-can cathedrals and tinfoil highways with maggots trundling along them like cars. Thousands of tiny people with bright-green hair were living inside it.

Sasha waved a hand to get his attention. "Max?"

"Yes?"

"There are green people in the bin."

"I'm looking at them, Sasha."

There was a long pause. Sasha waved again.

". . . Max?"

"Yes?"

"You might want to look at the bed while you're at it."

Max turned round. Underneath the bed—almost completely hidden from sight—was another city. It was *huge,* bigger than the castle and the bin city combined. It was filled with thousands of tiny red huts that spread the length of the bed frame, from headboard to footboard.

Standing inside it were hundreds of thousands of tiny people with bright-red hair, staring at them.

"Max?"

"Yes?"

"There are red people too."

"Yes."

"Loads of them."

"Yes."

"There could be *millions* of people in this room."

"Probably."

Pause.

"So . . . how *exactly* are we going to get them to our dorm?"

Max looked around the enormous room. He didn't know the answer to Sasha's question, but he knew one thing for certain.

Mr. Darrow hadn't just given him a kingdom to look after. He'd given him an entire *civilization*.

"We're going to need a bigger spade," said Max.

CHAPTER 16

Luke had never seen so many flies before. Sometimes you might see one or two, buzzing at the top of the ceiling, but now the Bin Kingdom was thick with them. There must have been hundreds.

"*War?* Malcolm, what do you—"

"*Get down!*"

Luke ducked behind the cage just as a huge fly circled the city walls. He recognized the droning buzz he'd heard filling the desert earlier.

"*Warflies,* Your Highness," Malcolm whispered. "The Bin King has been secretly breeding them for weeks! We knew he'd been using them to spy on us from the ceiling, but we had no idea he had something like *this* planned...."

This was no ordinary fly—it was more like a flying fortress. Its sides were wrapped in tinfoil armor, and strapped to its back were catapults and slingshots and trebuchets. Twenty Green soldiers stood behind the weapons, surveying the ground below.

"They hit us right after Demon left," Malcolm explained, "when we were at our most frightened and vulnerable. Three dozen warflies attacked the kingdom at once. We didn't stand a chance! They defeated our army, ransacked the city and sent the Blues marching to the Bin in chains!"

Sure enough, Luke could see a great crowd of blue on the other side of the desert.

"But why did they attack?" he whispered. "We've never done anything to the Greens!"

Malcolm's face darkened.

"It was all Demon's doing, Your Highness! When he appeared through the Bedroom Door, the Bin King sent two warflies to get a closer look and report their findings. One of them flew too close to Demon's accomplice, and the purple monster attacked without warning, crushing the warfly in midair!"

Luke gasped. "He killed a Green soldier?"

Malcolm shook his head. "The fly rider made a lucky escape, landing on the second warfly as he plummeted to the ground. He was carried back to the Bin in a terrible state, and was able to tell the Bin King everything he had seen: Demon kneeling down before you in the desert and talking to you; another monster appearing through the Door; you fleeing the city just before the Bin King's warfly was attacked. . . ."

Luke's stomach dropped. "No . . . you don't mean—"

"Yes! The Bin King thought *you* commanded those monsters to attack!" Malcolm cried. "He thought it was a declaration of war!"

Luke was aghast. "But that's insane!"

Malcolm shook his head. "The Bin King is a paranoid tyrant—it was all the excuse he needed. He's always wished to rule the entire Floor himself: your father and the Red Queen were able to keep him in line, but once King Adam died, we were certain the Greens would try to attack. That's why we had to crown you so quickly—we thought that without a king on the Blue throne, the Bin King would finally take his chance!"

Luke stared at the devastation around them.

"So . . . what do we do now?"

"There's nothing we *can* do, Luke!" Malcolm wailed. "The Blues are defeated! The Bin King will surely attack the Reds next—they may be the largest tribe on the Floor, but they're little more than disorganized savages. They'll be *nothing* against the might of the Bin King's warflies! The Red Queen will fall, and when she does, the Greens will rule from wall to wall! The Bin King won't rest until he has your head on a spike!"

Luke wasn't listening to Malcolm anymore. He was

looking at the remains of his kingdom. He had asked the Great One to take it away from him ... and gotten exactly what he had wished for. Because of him, thousands of men, women and children had been enslaved.

"What have I done?" he whispered.

Luke's eyes filled with tears. He had failed the very people he was sworn to protect. There was no way he could ever undo what had been done.

A shadow fell across him.

The Bedroom Door was opening again. The giants stood in the Doorway.

"D-Demon has returned!" Malcolm cried. "Run, Your Majesty, before it's too late!"

But Luke stayed where he was, staring up at the giants' faces. They were looking at the Floor, taking in what had happened ... and they were horrified.

They weren't monsters. They were just like Luke.

Except I'm a tiny boy, thought Luke, *and they're two giants who can crush whole cities with one hand....*

And all of a sudden, Luke knew exactly what he had to do.

CHAPTER 17

"Max! Look!"

Sasha was pointing at the model castle.

"I can see two blue people—right there, at the top of the big tower!"

Max squinted. He could just about make them out, too—two blues, standing beside the flagpole and talking to each other at superfast speed.

"Hey! It's the king we saw earlier!" said Max. "And that's the old man! It looks like he's in a cage." He paused. "Except . . . I don't think he's wearing any clothes."

Sasha made to step forward, but Max stopped him.

"Don't! We might frighten them—we can't let them run off like the others. I've got an idea."

He grabbed the microscope goggles from the desk.

"I'll see if I can lip-read what they're saying with these. Maybe we'll get some clues about what's going on."

Sasha was impressed. "You can lip-read?"

Max blinked. "Well, yeah, of course. I have to. I've been doing it my whole life."

"So you can tell what people are saying, even if they're far away?"

Max shook his head. "It's not that easy. You have to be able to see the mouth clearly, and even if you *can*, it's still easy to make mistakes."

But Sasha was still amazed. "Cool! It's like you have a superpower!"

Max flushed with pride.

"Well, I guess it's *kind* of like a superpower."

He pulled on the goggles, still blushing, and turned back to the castle. The tiny boy swung into view.

It was the first time Max had seen the king up close. He could make out every strand of his bright-blue hair, and the exact shade of his bright-blue eyes, and the grains of sand that dusted his robes. . . .

And that wasn't *all* he could see.

Sasha tapped him on the shoulder. "Can you see him?"

Max paused.

"Er . . . yeah. He's looking this way."

"Oh," said Sasha. "What's he doing?"

Max sought to find the right words.

"He's, er . . . he's *waving* at us."

• • •

"Luke! What are you doing?"

Luke stood at the tower's edge, waving at the giants.

"What does it look like I'm doing? I'm getting their attention!"

It was working. The first giant was staring down at him through his great stalk eyes. Luke could see each blink captured in slow motion through the glass, like the petals of a flower closing.

"His attention?!" cried Malcolm. "Why do you want his attention? He's Demon! He's a monster who wants to destroy the world!"

Luke shook his head. "I don't think he *is* Demon. He could have squashed me in a heartbeat earlier if he wanted to—both of them could have. They're not monsters. I think they're ... something else."

"Like what?!"

Luke shrugged. "I'm going to find out."

He stepped back, took a deep breath and spoke as loudly as he could.

"GREETINGS, GIANT! I AM LUKE, KING OF THE BLUES! DO YOU UNDERSTAND ME?"

Malcolm was horrified. "Luke, stop!"

"We have to tell them what's happened, Malcolm— they might be the only ones who can help us. GREET-INGS, GIANT! I AM LUKE, KING OF THE BLUES! DO YOU UNDERSTAND ME?"

Giant stared at him blankly through the lenses. Luke could see that he was struggling to make sense of what he was saying. Luke gritted his teeth—he had to keep trying. He spoke again, moving his mouth as slowly as possible.

"GREETINGS, GIANT! I AM LUKE, KING OF THE BLUES—"

"Technically, Your Highness, you're not king of the Blues until after the coronation ceremony, so—"

"Malcolm?"

"Yes?"

"Shut up. GREETINGS, GIANT! I AM LUKE, KING OF THE BLUES! DO YOU UNDERSTAND ME? GREETINGS, GIANT! I AM . . ."

• • •

Max couldn't believe it. "Hey—his lips are moving! He's trying to *talk* to us!"

Sasha gasped. "No way! What's he saying?"

Max squinted . . . and then his face fell.

"I don't know—he's talking too fast! It's like trying to read a river!"

Sasha groaned. "What about the old man? Is he talking?"

Max shook his head. "He's got a beard—that makes it even harder to read his lips."

Sasha studied the goggles.

"What if you zoomed in on their mouths? Would that make it easier?"

Max was unconvinced. "Mr. Darrow never taught me how to zoom in."

"Well, *one* of those buttons has to do something—there's loads of them!" said Sasha. "Look, there's one with an X on it, like the one on your hearing aid! Why don't we try it?"

Max shifted uncomfortably. "I'm not sure we should be pressing anything, Sasha; we're supposed to be looking after Mr. Darrow's things for him, not—"

Sasha jabbed the button. Max jumped.

"What did you do that for?"

"Well, we've got to try *something*."

"So? You could have broken them!" said Max. "And the goggles haven't zoomed in, they've just . . ."

Max trailed off. A fly had flown past. It was magnified hugely through the goggles; Max could see every hair on its body, every bump on the surface of its eyes.

He could also see that it was barely moving.

The fly hung suspended in the air, each beat of its wings moving with the grace of a ballerina. Standing on its back were twenty green soldiers pointing at Max and screaming in terror. But the tiny soldiers weren't super fast anymore—they all moved at normal speed.

Max took off the goggles. The fly buzzed to the other side of the room in a flash.

"What's wrong?" said Sasha. "Have I broken them?"

Max handed the goggles to Sasha, grinning from ear to ear. "See for yourself."

Sasha pulled the goggles on . . . and his mouth fell open.

"Nooooooo waaaaaay!"

Max nodded with excitement. "They're not just microscope goggles—they also slow everything down! Mr. Darrow must have added that button so he could see at the same speed as the tiny people!"

Sasha handed the goggles back to Max. "How about now? Can you read their lips?"

Max pulled the goggles back on and focused on the boy's face. All the boy's movements were slowed down now. Even better, he was speaking clearly enough for Max to understand what he was saying.

"Yes, it's working! He's calling me Giant—and his name is Luke! He's the king of the Blues . . . he's asking if we understand him!"

"Tell him our names!" said Sasha excitedly.

"Good idea." Max cleared his throat. "ER . . . HELLO, LUKE. MY NAME IS MAX, AND THIS IS SASHA. WE'RE ROOMMATES."

There was a pause.

"Did it work?" said Sasha. "What's he saying?"

Max watched for a while.

" 'My ears, for Great One's sake, my ears, Malcolm, calm down, Demon is trying to kill us all with his bellowing voice, I told you he's not trying to kill us, my ears, my ears, look, Giant, you're going to have to talk quicker or something, we can't understand a word you're saying, I think I've gone deaf, oh shut up, Malcolm.' "

Sasha grimaced. "Well, at least now we know the other one's called Malcolm."

Max pulled off the goggles.

"It's no use—everything about us must be super slow to them, including our voices!"

He stared down at the tiny boy on the tower.

"We *have* to keep him talking—it's our only chance of finding out what's happened. But how can we show him we understand? How can we talk to him without using our voices, or . . ."

And then Max realized what to do.

• • •

Luke's head was reeling. It was the second time he had been shouted at by Giant, and he hadn't enjoyed it the first time. The force of Giant's voice had blasted his hair into spikes, and Malcolm's beard was in even worse shape. It looked like he'd gone to a costume party dressed as a hedge and got beaten up on the way.

"Luke, what's he doing? I can't see a thing!"

Malcolm was trying to make a hole in his beard big enough to see through, without success. Luke gazed up at Giant groggily.

"He's . . . he's holding one hand to his head," he said.

That was it. Giant was sitting there with one hand cupped around his ear, looking at Luke expectantly.

"Luke, this is ridiculous!" said Malcolm. "He clearly doesn't understand a word you're saying. Stop talking to him and get us out of here!"

Luke kept his eyes fixed on Giant.

"No. It . . . it's like he's trying to tell us something. It's like he's saying . . ."

And suddenly Luke understood. His face broke into a smile.

"He wants me to keep talking. He wants to know what's going on."

Luke laughed in amazement. He never thought it would happen—but there it was, for the first time in his life.

"He . . . he's listening. *He's listening!*"

CHAPTER 18

Max sat with one hand cupped over his ear and his eyes on Luke's lips.

"It worked! He's talking again! He's explaining what happened!"

Max watched closely, nodding along as Luke spoke.

"He says that his people—the Blues—were attacked by . . . the Greens. Those must be the green-haired people in the bin. Something about . . . the flies doing it. *Warflies,* I think he's calling them. That must be the people I saw riding that fly a moment ago!"

Sasha frowned. "But why did the Greens attack? Did the Blues do something wrong?"

Max kept his eyes fixed on Luke.

"He . . . he says it's because of us! Because you attacked one of the warflies!" Max gasped. "That fly you swatted earlier must have had people on it!"

Sasha looked down at his onesie. There, just beside the zipper, was the squashed fly. He picked something out from the remains.

It was a tiny ejector seat.

"Aaaaargh!" cried Sasha.

Max turned back to the tower. "Wait—Luke says the pilot was fine! But the leader of the Greens—the Bin King—thought Luke told you to destroy the warfly, and that's why he attacked!"

Sasha turned pale. "You mean all this is my fault? Oh *man . . ."*

Max kept his eyes on the tower.

"And Luke says now it's just going to get worse! He says the Bin King is going to attack the Reds—those must be the red-haired people under the bed—and he's going to take over the whole floor! And the only thing that can stop him is . . ."

Max stopped. Through the goggles, he could see the desperation in Luke's eyes, clear as day. He'd never spoken to someone who was so easy to read before.

"Is what?" said Sasha.

Max smiled.

"Is *us*. He's asking us to help him."

• • •

"Did you understand me?"

Luke waited for Giant's response. Like everything Giant did, it took a while for the answer to come. You just had to wait.

And then, it came. Luke saw the exact moment that his words sank in. It was like watching a stone being dropped in a lake, and the ripples spreading out across the surface.

Giant's eyes flashed with understanding. The muscles of his mouth softened. His head rose ... and fell.

A nod.

"Is that a yes?" cried Luke. "You understand me? You'll help us?"

The head rose and fell once more—another nod. Luke leapt for joy.

"Malcolm, this is our chance! We can save the Blues— with Giant on our side, we'll be unstoppable!"

Malcolm had finally burrowed a hole through his beard big enough for him to see through.

"Fine!" he grumbled. "We'll use Demon to defeat the Bin King. Now for heaven's sake, offer him a blood sacrifice before he kills us."

Luke blinked. "A blood sacrifice?"

"Monsters need blood sacrifices to keep them

happy," Malcolm explained. "Offer him a thousand Greens to start with."

Luke was horrified. "We can't kill a thousand Greens!"

"Do you want to save the Blues or don't you?" Malcolm snapped.

Luke gulped, and turned back to Giant.

"Er ... thanks, Giant. We're very grateful. Do you want us to sacrifice a thousand Greens in your honor?"

Giant took a moment to listen, then grimaced. He shook his head.

"Pah!" said Malcolm. "He's holding out for more, the bloodthirsty brute! Right, we'll go up to five thousand— but that's our final offer."

Luke sighed. "Giant, what *do* you want?"

Giant held out his empty hands.

"Nothing?" said Luke. "Then ... why are you helping us?"

Giant looked confused, like he didn't know how to explain himself. Then his eyes lit up. He pointed to himself, and then at Luke. He held up his index fingers and crossed them over each other.

Luke frowned. "It looks like ... an X."

"That's ten in Roman numerals," said Malcolm. "Good grief—he wants ten thousand sacrifices! Right, offer him seven and a half, but tell him we'll have to do it in installments."

Luke looked at Giant, who still had his fingers crossed. It was like a hug or a handshake.

"I don't think that's what he means. I think . . . I think that sign means he wants to be *friends*. Is that right, Giant?"

Giant nodded, and Luke laughed. The two of them . . . well, it was like they just *understood* each other. Luke couldn't believe it—a whole lifetime with no one to talk to except for his pet flea, and here he was making friends with someone a hundred times bigger than him.

"Tell him we'll sacrifice two and a half thousand up front, then two and a half more on delivery of the Bin King, and then—"

"Malcolm?"

"Yes?"

"Shut up."

• • •

"Hey, that's the sign language I showed you!" said Sasha. "Friends, right?"

Max nodded, holding out his crossed fingers. He had never imagined that the first time he used sign language would be to talk to a boy who was smaller than his pinkie fingernail.

"I'm telling Luke we want to help him, that we're on his side! Maybe then he'll stop offering us sacrifices."

"*Sacrifices?*" said Sasha. "Wow, these guys are monsters."

Max looked down at the tiny boy. It was strange—he'd always found it hard to make friends, but in less than an hour, he'd made two. It was amazing what happened when you talked to people.

Sasha waved a hand in front of Max's face.

"Max, I don't mean to be difficult, but how *are* we going to help him? We're supposed to be getting everyone out of the room before Pitt comes back!"

Max looked around the room. Once again, Sasha was right. There were millions of people to save, and he and Sasha still didn't have anywhere to put them. Not only that—*now* the tiny people were at war. Even if Max and Sasha found a way to get everyone downstairs, the little people could end up slaughtering each other the moment they did.

"We have to stop them fighting first," said Max. "We need someone to take charge. Someone to talk to everyone and bring them together."

Max looked down at Luke and smiled.

"We need a *king*."

"Malcolm, look! Giant's trying to tell us something!"

Giant was pointing to himself, then across the desert, at the Bin Kingdom.

"You're going to destroy the Bin Kingdom?" said Luke. "Is that right?"

Giant scrunched up his face and shook his head. He pointed across the desert again, harder. He wasn't pointing at the Bin—he was pointing at the crowd of Blues outside it.

"You're going to get the Blues back for us?"

Giant nodded with relief.

"Well, I guess that's better than nothing." Luke smiled. "Thank you, Giant! We'll take it from there—we'll reorganize the army, attack the Greens ourselves and . . ."

He trailed off. Giant was shaking his head again. Luke thought he detected a look of disapproval in his eyes.

"You *don't* want us to attack the Greens?" said Luke.

Giant nodded. He pointed at Luke, then at the Bin, and locked his fingers together—X. Luke gawped.

"You want us to be *friends* with them?"

"*What?!*" said Malcolm. "Make an alliance with the tribe that just *attacked* us?"

Giant nodded. He pointed to Luke again, then

pointed behind him. In the distance stretched a flat-topped mountain with thousands of red-roofed huts sprawled beneath it. It was the Bed—the Red Kingdom. Giant locked his fingers together into another X.

"You want us to be friends with the Reds, too?" said Luke.

"*Those bloodthirsty savages?!*" cried Malcolm.

Giant nodded. He waved his hands across the entire Floor and then drew them back to himself, like he was sweeping everything together, Reds and Greens and Blues. Then he locked his fingers together again. Luke was amazed.

"He . . . he wants us to stop fighting. He wants us to come together as one tribe!" Luke looked up at Giant. "But how? Who's going to make an alliance with the Red Queen? Who's going to persuade the Bin King to stop fighting us? Who's going to—"

Luke stopped. Giant was pointing at him.

"*Me?!*"

Giant gave him a thumbs-up that was bigger than the tower Luke stood on.

• • •

"You really think that'll work?" said Sasha.

Max nodded, still giving Luke a thumbs-up.

"We'll take the Blues downstairs like we planned. By the time we come back up here, Luke will have talked to the Reds and Greens and explained what we're doing. That means we can carry them down one tribe at a time, and they won't try to kill each other when we reunite them!"

Sasha looked unconvinced. "Are you *sure* he'll be able to do all that?"

"Of course!" said Max. "He's a king, isn't he?"

He turned toward the boy on the tower. The whole fate of the floor rested on his tiny shoulders.

"Goodbye, King Luke," Max whispered. "And good luck."

• • •

Luke waved. "Goodbye, Giant!"

Luke watched as Giant slowly turned away. Malcolm looked like he had aged a hundred days in a second.

"Your Majesty, you cannot be serious! Make peace with the Greens after what they've done? Form an alliance with the Reds?"

Luke nodded. "This is it, Malcolm, the answer to everything! No more fighting, no more tribes ... no more squabbling over food and territory! And Giant and his friend are going to help us achieve it!"

Malcolm was appalled. "The Bin King is looking for you as we speak—he'll cut your head off the moment he finds you! As for the Red Queen, you won't get within a foot of the Red Kingdom before those savages tear you limb from limb!"

Luke wasn't listening. He was already turning away to face the vast, sprawling sands that lay ahead.

"Remember what you told me earlier, Malcolm? Everyone gets one chance: one moment to prove themselves."

He picked up his crown and sword.

"Well, this is mine. Now I understand why I never wanted to be king. My job isn't to rule people—it's to save the Floor. And not just for the Blues, for *everyone*."

Malcolm sputtered like a faulty kettle. "Luke, your father would never have—"

"I already told you," said Luke. "I'm not my father."

He swung his sword at the cage and split the lock in two. The door fell open. Malcolm was stunned.

"Luke, you're acting like . . ."

"I know," said Luke, smiling. "A king."

With that, he flew down the stairs and out into the desert. There was nothing Malcolm could do except stand speechless in his underpants and watch as Luke leapt onto Excelsior's back far below him. She reared up onto her hind legs, and the two of them bounded toward the horizon. Gradually, inch by inch, Luke disappeared—away from his past and his kingdom, and on toward his destiny.

CHAPTER 19

Max watched the blue dot race across the sand.

"Come on, we don't have much time!" Sasha clapped him on the back. "Let's grab the Blues and get them downstairs!"

Max didn't answer. He was thinking about something Mr. Darrow had said to him once.

The janitor had been fixing his latest model: a scale replica of Buckingham Palace, with 775 rooms and seventy-eight working toilets. It had taken him a whole year to build, but now he was taking it apart again. He'd discovered a mistake in his calculations, and one of the bedroom walls was a millimeter off.

"Why bother?" said Max. "It's only a millimeter!"

Mr. Darrow looked at him through the microscope goggles. Beneath the glass lenses, his eyes were magnified to fat black beetles.

"Do you like poetry, Max?"

Max thought about it. "Er . . . I think so."

"Well, I don't," said Mr. Darrow. "It's just writing with bits missing. Laziness, if you ask me." He leaned over the palace with a pair of tweezers. "But there's one poem I *do* like:

'To see the world in a grain of sand,
And heaven in a wild flower,
Hold infinity in the palm of your hand
And eternity in an hour . . . '"

Max frowned. "What does that mean?"

Mr. Darrow took hold of the faulty wall.

"It means you have to find beauty in the smallest things—because small things are important. If you don't take care of them, they come back to bite you."

He pulled out the faulty wall . . . and the whole palace collapsed. He held up the tiny piece of wood. It was no bigger than a splinter, but it had held everything together.

"Never forget that, Max," he said. "A millimeter matters."

Max watched as Luke disappeared across the floor. Just like the single piece of wood in Mr. Darrow's model, everything relied on him now. If he didn't succeed in making peace with the Reds and Greens, then there was no way that Max's plan would work.

Sasha stepped toward the bin, but once again Max stopped him.

"No! Not so fast!"

Sasha blinked. "Why not?"

"Because we have to get this *perfect*." He held out his arms to the room. "Look around you—all this started because of one squashed fly!"

Sasha looked guilty. "I told you, that was an accident. . . ."

"Of course it was!" said Max. "But we can't let anything else go wrong now—we have to make sure we do this without anyone getting hurt."

Sasha gulped. "How are we going to free the Blues without hurting any Greens?"

They looked at the crowd of Blues outside the Bin. The Greens had already put them to work constructing a giant papier-mâché monument of the Bin King from old newspaper. Green soldiers on warflies were whipping the Blues with strands of dental floss.

"We have to get the Greens to leave," said Max. "But no scaring them! They all think we're monsters, so we have to show them we're not!"

Max picked up the shovel and the two boys carefully

crept toward the Bin, checking with every footstep to make sure they didn't accidentally squash anyone.

"That's it, nice and slow," said Max. "Show the Greens that we're not here to hurt them and—"

Max stopped. The Greens had already panicked and shot inside the Bin, barricading the entrance with two empty crisp packets. The imprisoned Blues were left stranded on the sand, staring up at Max and Sasha in terror.

"Never mind," said Max. "Let's just grab them."

He pulled on the goggles and crouched in front of the Blues, who were cowering and begging for their lives.

"Don't be afraid!" said Max. "I'm not going to hurt you—just stay still!"

He carefully dug the shovel into the sand beneath the Blues and then lifted it as slowly as he could. It was trickier than Max had expected—he was petrified that at any moment the Blues would panic, charge off the shovel and fall to their deaths—but when he finally stood up, he was relieved to see it had gone perfectly. The Blues stood safe and sound in the middle of the shovel.

"Quick! The tray!"

Sasha held out the seedling tray, and Max deposited the sand inside. Ten thousand Blues tumbled across the plastic and squeaked in panic, but it looked like no one was hurt. Max breathed a sigh of relief and carried the tray to the desk.

"Right, almost done!" he said. "Bring me the castle and I'll get it fixed."

Sasha raised an eyebrow. "Fix the castle? Why?"

"The Blues need somewhere to live, remember?" said Max. "It's not big enough, but it's better than nothing. I've got to make sure the castle is safe—they could trip on the broken staircases, or get skewered on splinters or crushed by falling roof beams, or—"

"All right, all right," Sasha grumbled. "Just be quick—we're running out of time!"

Max carried the castle to the desk and pulled off the base with a set of Mr. Darrow's precision tweezers. Malcom was no longer anywhere to be seen, but Max could see all the damage done in the battle. There were doors broken in, and tiny scuff marks on the walls from miniature sword fights. Sasha tapped him on the shoulder.

"Max, you *made* that?"

Max nodded.

"I had no idea you were so good!" Sasha shook his head in amazement. "Why didn't you tell me?"

Max tried not to blush, and failed. "I thought you'd think making models was, you know . . . stupid."

"Are you kidding? I could never make *anything* as good as that!"

Max shrugged. "So? You're good at talking to people—I'd give anything to do that."

Sasha handed him the glue, and Max started fixing the broken doors.

"You know, Max, you're too hard on yourself," said Sasha. "You should try talking to people more."

Max shook his head. "I'm no good with people."

"You're good with *me*."

Max snorted. "Yeah, but you're *easy* to talk to! Most people aren't. Can you pass me the tweezers?"

Sasha handed them over. "You can't be on your own all the time. Why don't you start a model-making club here? Show people what you can do—I bet loads of kids would want to learn."

Max shook his head.

"It's a nice idea, but it's not for me. Half the time I've got no idea what people are saying. That's why I've always loved models, you know? You don't have to struggle to understand models. They just *are*."

He put the base back on the castle and started filling the holes in the walls.

"I guess I've never had much control over anything in my life. But when I'm making models, I'm in charge—even if it's just for a short while. It feels good. In fact, it's the only thing I've ever been good at."

He fixed the turrets on the towers so each one stood up straight.

"That's why we have to get this *perfect*. This is my

chance to show Mr. Darrow I'm good enough to look after his work for him. After this, who knows . . . maybe we can start up a business or something. Me and him, making living models together."

Max put the castle on the desk and admired it. It was already as good as new.

"There!" He dusted off his hands. "Now let's get these Blues downstairs, before—"

"*Max!*"

Sasha was frantically waving at him, pointing at the tray in horror.

"*The flies!*"

Max gasped. Hundreds of warflies were pouring from the bin behind him and landing on the tray. Green soldiers were grabbing as many Blues as they could, dragging them onto the flies and carrying them away by the dozen.

"They're taking the Blues!" Max cried. "Stop them!"

Sasha ran in front of the bin, blocking a swarm of flies as they tried to reenter it—and leapt back.

"Ow! They just stung me!"

"*Stung* you? How could a fly—"

Max felt a sudden sharp pain on his cheek and yelped. One of the warflies circled his head. With the goggles, Max could see Green soldiers on its back loading up their catapults with tiny staples broken into razor-sharp fragments.

"They're—ow!—firing at us!" said Max.

"You think?" cried Sasha, swatting flies left and right. "Go away! Shove it, you stupid little—"

"No!" cried Max. "There are—ow!—people riding them, remember? You can't hurt them! Keep blocking the bin and I'll—ow!—save the Blues!"

He reached down to scoop the rest of the Blues from the tray, but he was too late. The Blues didn't want to be saved—they were running from him. Some were even climbing onto the warflies to escape, hugging the Green captors and crying with relief as they were carried away.

"No! What are you doing?" said Max. "Don't go with the Greens—they're the enemy! I'm trying to save you!"

It was no good—the Blues didn't understand. Within seconds they had fled the tray, and a swarm of warflies surrounded Max and Sasha, flinging round after round of catapult fire at their faces.

"Max! What do we do?"

Max gazed around the room in horror. Mr. Darrow's creation was even less like a model than he'd thought. It couldn't be controlled at all. It fought back.

There was only one thing to do now.

"RUUUUN!"

Max and Sasha leapt out the door, slamming it behind them. They stood in the corridor, gasping for breath.

"That went well," said Sasha.

His face was covered with so many swollen marks it looked like he'd nose-dived in a bowl of red jelly beans.

"Right, forget being nice!" he said, rolling up his sleeves. "Let's go back in there and show those Greens what we're made of!"

Max held him back. "No! We can't hurt them!"

"Why not? They're hurting us!"

"Because it's Mr. Darrow's creation, remember? We can't damage it—not even one person! Mr. Darrow always used to tell me that even the smallest things matter: you take your attention away for one second, and before you know it, they—"

Max stopped. He had noticed something from the corner of one eye.

Joy and the Sparkle Pony Summer Club were standing at the top of the stairs, staring at them.

"J-Joy!" cried Sasha. "What are you doing up here? I told you not to leave the games room!"

Joy was surprised. "We came to look for you. You said you'd be gone only a little while. . . ."

"Well, we're done now!" said Sasha. "Get downstairs, before Mr. Pitt—"

"What were you doing in Mr. Darrow's room?"

Max and Sasha froze.

"Wh-what?" said Max.

"We just saw you come out of Mr. Darrow's room," said Joy.

Max and Sasha shared a terrified glance.

"We weren't doing anything!" said Sasha. "So don't tell anyone, OK? Especially not Mr. Pitt!"

Max winced—Sasha had already said too much. Joy's eyes lit up. A smile tweaked at the corner of her mouth.

"Soooo . . . you're saying that if Mr. Pitt found out, you two would be in trouble?"

Sasha nodded. "Yes! Lots of trouble!"

Joy walked toward them, playing with her pigtails innocently. "Soooo . . . if we decided to tell him, then you two would be expelled?"

Sasha's face turned white as he realized what was happening. All the girls were walking toward them now, smiling.

"Joy, please! This is important—you *have* to believe me!"

Joy shook her head sadly. "But how *can* I believe you, Sasha? You said you'd spend the whole day with me, but you didn't. . . . You said we'd make friendship bracelets and do dance routines and watch *The Sparkle Pony Movie*, and we haven't done *any* of those things. . . ."

"We will!" said Sasha. "Max and I will do anything you want!"

Joy stopped—it was exactly what she had been waiting for. She turned to the girls behind her, and they grinned like a shoal of piranhas. Max suddenly felt very, very frightened.

"Anything?" said Joy.

CHAPTER 20

Luke stood beside the Bed. Ahead of him lay thousands of Red shacks, scattered on the sand like blood drops.

"We did it, Excelsior. We made it!"

The journey across the desert had been long and treacherous. Excelsior could clear whole dunes in a single bound, but with the warflies on the lookout, Luke had had no choice but to hide every few inches to avoid being seen. Once Giant and his friend left for the Bin, the warflies had disappeared—and Luke had taken his chance. He rode like the wind to the Red Kingdom, stopping only to break into some abandoned houses along the way and put together a cunning disguise.

Luke knew he didn't have much time—once Giant had saved the Blues, the Bin King was sure to attack again. He had to find the Red Queen, explain everything to her and get her on his side—fast.

There was just one problem: he had no idea where she was.

Luke stared hopelessly at the sea of Red shacks. There was nothing that looked even *remotely* like someplace a queen would live. He needed to ask for directions, but everyone knew the Reds hated the Blues. If anyone found out who he was, they'd beat the living daylights out of him.

He looked at the nearest building: a Red saloon, right on the outskirts of town. It looked ... rough. The sort of place whose patrons would happily rip off his arms and legs and hit him with them. But it also looked like the sort of place where people didn't ask too many questions. Someone in there was *bound* to tell him where the Red Queen was.

Plus, it smelled like there was *food* inside.

Luke's stomach groaned. He'd never gone so long without eating before. In Blue Castle, he had only to snap his fingers and someone would come running with a tray of the finest crumbs. Now he was on a quest to save the whole Floor, and he'd never been so hungry. He tied Excelsior to a post and patted her side.

"Wait here, girl," he said. "I won't be long."

Excelsior chirruped happily. Luke tried to look brave for her, but he knew the truth. If he let his disguise slip for a moment—if *anyone* suspected he wasn't a Red—he'd never get out of the saloon alive. He gave his disguise a final tweak, adopted what he thought was a tough stance and strolled through the doors.

It was dark and dingy inside. There was a cluster of tables with some miserable-looking Reds slumped over their drinks. Everyone seemed thin and pale and sick. Luke spotted a man at a table near him, drinking alone. He slapped the man on the back.

"Greetings, fellow Red! I'm trying to find the Red Queen—do you know where she lives?"

The man looked confused. Luke froze—of course the man didn't understand him. He was supposed to be talking like a Red.

"I mean . . . all right, mate! I'm trying to find the Red Queen, innit? Any idea where her gaff might be?"

The man stared at Luke for a long time before he answered.

"Are you wearing a bucket on your head?"

Luke's face drained. He'd had no idea that the thing on his head was a bucket. He'd thought it was some kind of rustic peasant hat.

"Are you all right?" said the man. "You're sweating a lot. You should probably take off that dressing gown."

This wasn't going well. People were beginning to look at him. Luke panicked.

"Er . . . no thanks, mate! In fact, I just realized I don't need any more help, mate! Bye! Mate!"

He fled to the bar and sat down with a groan. He had to face facts: he didn't know what he was doing. If he was going to find the Red Queen, he needed help—and lots of it.

"Can I help you?"

Luke looked up. There was a girl standing on the other side of the bar, polishing a glass. She was about his age, with bright-red eyes and bright-red hair tied in a ponytail and held in place with two small daggers. She also had a large club with a nail sticking out of it strapped to her back.

"Yes!" said Luke. "I'm trying to find the Red Queen. Do you know where she is? It's kind of a life-and-death situation."

The girl blinked.

"I just meant, like, a drink or something," she said.

Luke's stomach groaned again. "Do you have any food?"

She pointed to a jar on the counter. "I've got these old pickled flea eggs, but someone left them out under the Bulb, so I wouldn't . . ."

She didn't bother finishing the sentence. Luke was already swallowing the eggs six at a time.

"Hungry?" the girl asked.

Luke nodded as much as he could while fisting whole eggs into his mouth. The girl snorted.

"Well, you won't find the Red Queen now! She's busy preparing the Red Army for war. It's only a matter of time before the Greens try to attack us . . . if Demon doesn't get us first!" The girl shook her head. "Ever since he turned up, the whole Floor's gone mad. But it's not all bad, I guess; at least those Blues finally got what was coming to them!"

Luke stopped eating.

"Especially that spoiled wiener, Prince Luke," the girl continued. "Last thing I heard, he was on the run across the desert! Ha! That puny little sap won't last ten seconds without a fleet of servants wiping his bum for him!"

Luke chewed for a while before swallowing.

"Maybe he'll do really well," he said.

The girl frowned. "What do *you* care?"

"I—I don't!" said Luke. "I hate the Blues just as much as anyone else! It's just, you know, always worth questioning your sources, and so on." He grabbed another handful of eggs. "Plus, you have to admire Prince Luke's heroism, don't you? Going on a quest to single-handedly save the Floor, being the only one who realizes that Gi—I mean, *Demon's* not evil and making an alliance with him to save the Blues. . . . Certainly makes you question whether you should be calling him a wiener, doesn't it?"

The girl was confused. "What do you mean, 'save the Blues'? The warflies chased Demon and the other monster out of the room before they could even—"

Luke sprayed her with a mouthful of egg.

"They did *what?!*"

Luke's mind was reeling. The Greens had defeated Giant—his one and only ally against the Bin King was gone. Now he really *did* have to find the Red Queen fast, or else . . .

Luke paused. The girl was glaring at him, covered in egg.

"Sorry," he said.

"It's fine," said the girl, not meaning it. "Spit as much food as you want. You're paying for it."

Luke's face fell. ". . . Paying?"

"Yes," said the girl. "This is a bar. We sell food and beverages in exchange for money."

Luke panicked. He'd never had to pay for anything in his life.

"Oh! *Paying!* Of course! Er . . . unfortunately, I've left all sacks of gold at home. How much do I owe for the eggs—ten thousand? A hundred thousand?"

The girl gave him a long, hard look.

"You know what—forget it. It's on me." She handed him a bottle. "Here, have a drink, too. My name's Ivy."

Luke smiled. "Wow, thank you, Ivy!"

"You're welcome, Prince Luke."

Luke managed to take a sip before he realized what she'd said. He choked on the drink and tried to run, but Ivy had already whipped one of the daggers out of her hair and pinned him to the bar by his sleeve.

"You know, I *thought* I recognized you when you walked in," she said cheerily. "But I never thought you'd be so stupid as to walk into a Red saloon wearing *that* outfit. A bucket and a dressing gown? What were you thinking?"

"I—I don't know what you're talking about!" cried Luke, trying to free himself. "I'm just your average Red, trying to—"

"Give it up," said Ivy. "I can see your blue hair under the bucket. And—hang on—are you still wearing your *crown*? Oh, this is priceless!"

Luke leaned close to whisper. "Ivy, please, you have to let me go! I need to find the Red Queen!"

"Oh, don't worry, I'll let you find her!" said Ivy. "Right after I rip off your arms and legs and hit you with them—"

"*Ahem.*"

The voice came from behind Luke, who had never

actually heard someone say *Ahem* before. Whatever it meant, though, it was highly effective. The entire saloon was silenced. Even Ivy stopped talking. Luke tore his sleeve free, made to run—and stopped.

There were ten Green soldiers in the doorway. A fly rider stood in front of them, smiling at the seated drinkers.

"Greetings."

All the Reds leapt to their feet at the same time, their chairs scraping across the floor. The fly rider waved his hands.

"Please, sit down," he said. "We come in peace!"

The Reds stayed on their feet. The fly rider glanced over them.

"Who owns this saloon?"

"I do."

Luke spun round in surprise—Ivy had her hand up and was meeting the fly rider's gaze head-on. The fly rider laughed.

"*You?* You're barely a week old! Where are your parents, little girl?"

"Dead," said Ivy. "Starved to death when I was five days old, along with thousands of other Reds after the Bin King raised food prices. What do you want?"

The fly rider's smile disappeared. He glanced at the other Reds. They looked like they were about to leap on the Greens and pummel them to dust, and the Greens knew it. The tension in the room was unbearable. The fly rider cleared his throat.

"I come with an offer from the Bin King himself." He started unrolling a poster. "He's prepared to pay a handsome reward to anyone who finds the cowardly traitor Prince Luke of the Blues!"

Luke nearly choked again. The poster was supposed to be of him, but whoever had drawn it had given him snake eyes and devil horns. He was standing on Giant's shoulders, controlling him with lightning bolts from his hands.

"He's the one who summoned Demon to the Floor, using evil Blue magic!" said the fly rider. "He longs to rule the Floor at any price! He even offered Demon his *own people* as a blood sacrifice, but when the monsters tried to take them from the heroic Greens, the might of the warflies sent them fleeing! The Bin King is determined to bring Luke to justice. Come forward with any information of his whereabouts and you shall be richly rewarded!"

Luke closed his eyes, waiting for the moment when Ivy would hand him over. The fly rider cleared his throat.

"The Bin King has *another* offer too. An even more generous one."

He began to stalk between the tables.

"The Green tribe is becoming stronger. The Blues are already defeated, and the age of the Green Floor will soon begin. If any Reds here wish to leave the Bed and join the Green tribe—to work as servants, of course—then the Bing King will guarantee them a life of plenty. They'll be given their own homes in the Bin, in the up-and-coming Banana Skin District, and provided with all the food they'll ever need. All you have to do is swear allegiance to the Bin King!"

The saloon was so silent you could hear dust settling on the tables. The Reds glanced at each other—Luke could see that some of them were tempted.

Ivy put a hand on his arm.

"We'll let you know if we see Prince Luke," she said to the fly rider. "As for your offer, thanks, but no thanks. The Reds will *never* bow down to the Bin King. Ever."

There was a mutter of angry agreement from the Reds, even the ones who'd looked tempted only a moment earlier. The fly rider glanced around the saloon and shrugged.

"Suit yourselves."

He turned to leave, then stopped.

"But I should point out ... the age of the Green Floor *is* coming. Do you really want to be on the wrong side of history when the inevitable happens? Because when it does, the Bin King will not look kindly on those who refused him."

"We'll keep that in mind," said Ivy.

The fly rider took one last look around the saloon, then stormed out. The Green soldiers followed. One by one, the Reds returned to their seats. But fear had filled the room like hot smoke. No one could doubt the meaning behind the fly rider's words: the Greens were going to attack. It was only a matter of time.

Luke turned to Ivy, dripping sweat. "Th-thank you."

"What for?"

"For not handing me over."

Ivy rolled her eyes. "Please—we Reds hate the Greens even more than we hate the Blues. There's no way we'd let the Bin King have you! But seeing as I *did* just save your life, I need a favor."

"Anything!"

"Turn around for a second."

Luke turned around. "Why? What's behind—"

Ivy whacked Luke on the head with her club, knocking him out cold. She slung his unconscious body over her shoulder and carried him out the door as easily as if he were a bag of rubbish.

"Honestly," she muttered. "What a wiener."

CHAPTER 21

Luke came to and looked blearily around him.

He was inside a Red shack. There wasn't much to look at, just a rough wooden table and a bed of rags in the corner.

Except, of course, for the drawings.

They covered the walls from floor to ceiling. They'd been drawn with ashes on cheap paper, but each was even more beautiful, intricate and detailed than the last. Every single one showed something with wings: drawings of flies, drawings of gnats, drawings of mosquitoes . . .

And right beside the bed was the biggest drawing of all. It showed a moth in flight, with a red-haired girl on its back. Two adults were holding her lovingly.

"Ah, good. You're awake."

Ivy stood behind him, sharpening her daggers.

"Thought you'd be out for a while longer. That crown must have protected your skull."

She nodded to Luke's crown, which lay on the floor beside her. It had been severely flattened by the club.

"My crown!" said Luke. "Give it back!"

He tried to grab it . . . but couldn't. He was tied to a chair.

"No chance," said Ivy. "You're staying right where you are while I put up the rest of these posters."

Ivy held one up. It was just as beautifully made as the drawings on the wall . . . but Luke didn't feel quite so positive about it.

ALWAYS WANTED TO PUNCH PRINCE LUKE IN THE FACE?

NOW'S YOUR CHANCE!

PRICE
1 HANDFUL OF FOOD = 1 PUNCH
2 HANDFULS = 3 PUNCHES

KIDS GO HALF PRICE!

"Like it?" said Ivy. "I wanted to put more decoration round the capitals, really make the letters pop, but I didn't have enough time."

Luke squirmed. "No—you have to let me go! I need to find the Red Queen!"

Ivy smiled. "Don't worry, you'll see her—right after

the first wave of punters. I've already sold a hundred tickets!"

She strode out the door. Luke sat up—he had one chance to get the girl's attention.

"The Greens are going to attack!" he cried. "And when they do, the Reds are done for!"

Ivy stopped and turned round.

"I'm sorry?"

"They defeated the Blue army in seconds," Luke said. "You don't stand a chance!"

Ivy snorted. "We Reds are made of stronger stuff than you think. If it comes to war—"

"It might not even come to that," said Luke. "The Greens attacked the Blues with three dozen warflies and won—there are *hundreds* more where those came from! There's only one way to stop the Bin King, and that's me. Keep me tied up here and the Reds are doomed!"

Ivy looked at him for a moment. She stepped back into the hut, pulled up a box and sat down.

"Tell me everything," she said.

Luke puffed out his chest. "I won't tell you a thing until you untie me!"

Ivy picked up her club.

"Tell me everything," she repeated.

"Of course," Luke squeaked.

He told her the whole story—how Giant and his friend had first appeared, how Luke had fled and the Greens had attacked, how Giant had offered to help him save the Blues. Ivy listened carefully.

"Everything that fly rider told you was a lie," Luke explained. "The Giant isn't Demon, and I don't control him with magic—the Bin King's just saying whatever he can to frighten the Reds into surrendering. I swear on my life, Ivy, I'm not lying to you!"

Ivy nodded. "I believe you."

Luke sighed with relief. "Thank you."

"You're not clever enough to lie," she said. "What I *really* want to know is this—if the Bin King's going to attack again, then what difference will it make for you to talk to the Red Queen?"

"We have to reunite the tribes," said Luke. "Like we were in the beginning, before everyone spread across the desert! It's the only way to stop the fighting. It won't be easy, but if the Red Queen and I can meet with the Bin King, then maybe we can both . . ."

He stopped. Ivy was cackling with laughter.

"What's so funny?"

"Reunite the tribes?" said Ivy. "Luke, the Bin King's not going to listen to peace now! And even if you had a

whole week, you'd *never* persuade the Reds to forgive the Blues for what they've done to us!"

Luke's face fell. "What have the Blues ever done to you?"

Ivy stared at him, shocked.

"Luke—look around. The Reds live in complete poverty. We give everything we have to the Greens in exchange for a morsel of rancid food. Did King Adam step in to help us when the Reds were starving to death? No, he just built walls around Blue Castle to keep us out. He's got blood on his hands—and that means you do, too."

Luke shifted on the chair. He hadn't known anything about that. He *really* wished he'd read more of those library books instead of falling asleep.

"Look," he said. "I don't blame you for hating the Blues—I would, too. But I'm not my father. And believe me, I'm not keen to make peace either. You really think I want to shake hands with the Bin King? He destroyed my kingdom and enslaved my people! He tried to have me killed!"

Ivy frowned. "Then why are you doing this?"

Luke sighed. "Because this is about saving the *whole* Floor. Everyone, even the people we don't want to. And besides, Giant says we should."

Ivy raised an eyebrow. "What is it with you and Giant?"

"He listens." Luke shifted on the chair again. "And ever since he spoke to me, I've been thinking about what reuniting the tribes would actually mean. The Bin King wouldn't control the food anymore. Everything would belong to everyone. There'd be no more fighting, no more starvation ... no more kings. Just one Floor, helping each other to survive. Doesn't that sound like something worth taking a risk for?"

Ivy's eyes flickered between Luke and her club.

"You really believe that could happen?"

"I do."

"It's completely mad."

"I know."

Ivy looked at him for some time, her eyes weighing it all. Finally she put down the club.

"Fine, you win. I'll help you stop the war."

Luke's heart filled with relief. "Really? You mean it?"

"Trust me, you need all the help you can get." She untied him. "But there's no point looking for the Red Queen. She's not going to listen to a word you say, and neither is the Bin King. You might have had a chance when everyone thought you controlled two huge monsters, but now that they're gone, you're about as scary as my grandmother."

Luke didn't know anything about Ivy's grandmother, but he imagined she was pretty terrifying.

"But there *is* someone who might listen to you," said Ivy. "Someone whose opinion people care about. And with him behind you, then who knows . . . you might just have half a chance!"

"Who?"

"Isn't it obvious?" said Ivy. *"The Wise Man!"*

Luke gawped. "The one from the Book of the Floor? Why?"

Ivy gave him a look. "You *have* read the Book of the Floor, haven't you?"

"Er . . . yeah, most of it," Luke lied.

Ivy walked to the shelves beside the bed and picked out a copy of the Book. It was very different from Luke's: while his had been made from the finest moth wings and bound with rare curtain fibers, Ivy's was cheap paper and had been opened and closed so many times that it barely held together.

"Here." She flipped to a page and handed the book to Luke. "Read that."

THE BOOK OF THE FLOOR

PART 3: THE RETURN OF THE WISE MAN

I.   After the tribes had scattered and settled in their new homes—the Reds under the Bed, the Greens in the Bin, and the Blues at the Castle—the Wise Man came looking for them. And to each tribe he said the same thing:

II.   "What are you doing? You were supposed to be exploring the flipping Floor, you idiots, not building different flipping kingdoms on different sides of the flipping room. We need to return as one tribe and work together, or we're well and truly stuffed."

III.   And at each kingdom, the people gave the same reply: "We shall not reunite, for us Reds/Greens/Blues will have nothing to do with the Reds/Greens/Blues." [Delete as applicable.]

IV.   To which the Wise Man said: "But we must work together to bring back the Great One. If we do not do it soon, then DEMON will come and destroy us all!"

V.   But the people did not listen. And so the Wise Man retreated to the desert and started his own tribe at the Holy Mountain: one where people were neither Red nor Green nor Blue. And there the Wise Man

busied himself for many weeks, searching the desert
for that which would bring the Great One back. . . .

Luke glanced up. "The Wise Man wanted to reunite
the tribes, too?"

Ivy nodded. "He's your answer—someone with clout.
After everything that's happened, people are bound to
listen to him! If we get the Wise Man on our side, then
there's a chance that the Red Queen and the Bin King
might listen to you, too!"

"But how do we find him?"

Ivy tapped the Book. "It says right there—the Holy
Mountain. And everyone knows how to find that: follow
the Sky Compass!"

She led Luke out of the shack and pointed high
above the desert. There, right in the center of the ceiling, was a huge four-pointed star.

"Reds have been using it to navigate the Floor
for weeks," said Ivy. "Head toward that, and we'll find
the Holy Mountain. We have to be quick, though—the
Greens could attack at any moment! It'd help if we had
a flea, or—"

Luke gasped. *"Excelsior!"*

They found the flea still tied up outside Ivy's saloon.
The moment she saw Luke, she growled, wriggling her
abdomen and stamping furiously. Luke gave her a hug.

"Oh, girl, don't look at me like that—I'd *never* leave you!" He tickled her thorax. "Who's the best flea? *Who's the best flea?*"

Ivy smiled. She handed Luke his crown and sword.

"Here, you can have these back now."

Luke was confused. "You're giving me back my sword?"

Ivy shrugged. "Anyone who's that nice to a flea has got to be OK."

Luke patted his steed lovingly. "Excelsior's more than just a flea—she's my best friend. I've had her ever since she was a pupa. I found her in the desert, all alone and half starved and—"

"Her name's not Excelsior."

"Huh?"

Ivy pointed at the flea's side. "See those markings? It means she's from Red territory—we mark all our fleas with symbols to show their breed and name. Her name's not Excelsior."

"Oh," said Luke. "What is it?"

Ivy read carefully.

"'Miss Binkles.'"

Luke was horrified. *"Miss Binkles?!"*

"Yep." Ivy leapt onto Miss Binkles's back. "Come on, Luke, we've got a war to stop! Remember, you don't have Giant helping you anymore. . . . It's all up to us!"

Luke climbed up beside Ivy. "See, *that's* the only bit I don't understand."

Luke gazed at the Bedroom Door, still closed on the farthest wall.

"Giant wants us to become one tribe, right? But *why*? And if he wants it so badly, then why isn't he still here, trying to help us?"

Luke shook his head.

"I mean, what could he be doing that's so important?"

CHAPTER 22

Max and Sasha were having makeovers.

The two boys were tied down to the Ping-Pong table. The Sparkle Pony Summer Club had been working their magic on them for some time: Max wore several layers of sparkly eye shadow, while Sasha had been bronzed a shade of orange called Luscious Carrot™.

"Joy, please! Let us go!" Sasha begged.

"Nuh-*uh*, Sasha!" Joy laughed. "You have to do everything we say, remember?" She started untying the ropes that held the boys to the table. "Girls, get the scissors! It's time to do their hair!"

The boys took their chance to escape. They flew out of the games room, the girls following close behind in a hurricane of glitter. They made it to their dorm just in time, slamming the door and shoving a chair under the handle. The girls clawed at the wood, hissing like cats and waving lipsticks menacingly under the frame.

"Wow, I've never seen them this bad before!" said Sasha. "At least all their candy's in here with us. If they had more sugar now, they'd probably . . ."

He stopped. Max was sitting on the edge of his bed, staring miserably at one of his fantasy books. The cover showed a battle between two kings—one good and one evil, their swords locked, surrounded by their ruined kingdoms and thousands of dead and wounded. He sighed.

"Look at us. Mr. Darrow's world is upstairs, fighting for survival. Millions of people are relying on us to come back." He threw the book across the room. "And we're stuck down here, getting our nails done by a bunch of five-year-old girls!"

Sasha sat beside him. "I know it's frustrating, but if Joy squeals on us, then Mr. Darrow's secret will be discovered *and* we'll be expelled!" He patted Max on the back. "We just have to wait till she's calmed down a little. Then we can go back upstairs."

"We don't have *time* for that!" Max groaned. "Don't you know about the butterfly effect?"

Sasha looked blank.

"Mr. Darrow told me about it," Max explained. "Imagine if, a thousand miles away, a butterfly flaps its wings. It doesn't affect us, right?"

Max spread his arms wide, holding them out to the room.

"But the world is made up of *trillions* of tiny things that are all connected to each other. That one small gust from the butterfly's wings could join up with another gust of wind, which travels up into the atmosphere and joins up with a billion more tiny bits of wind, and it grows and grows . . . until a thousand miles later, that one small gust has become a hurricane!"

"What's that got to do with us?" said Sasha.

"It means one small change can ruin *everything*. Think about it—we swatted a fly and it started a war. What if it keeps building? What if Luke fails and the Bin King takes over the floor, and it's all because of us?" He shook his head. "I can't let that happen. This is about more than keeping Mr. Darrow's secret safe—there's a whole world counting on us!"

Sasha groaned. "But even if we *could* get into Mr. Darrow's room, those flies are going to attack us again the second we step inside! What can we do?"

Max smiled. He reached into his pocket . . . and pulled out Mr. Darrow's microscope goggles.

"Do you have a phone?"

• • •

Mr. Pitt marched into the foyer of the Pitt Building. It was the stunning centerpiece of the new construction, with a polished wood floor, a high glass ceiling and a gigantic X-shaped walkway that ran from one side of the first floor to the other.

"Oi! Foreman!"

The foreman was talking to a handful of his exhausted workers. He had the look of a man who had spent several weeks being shouted at.

"What is it, D—I mean, Mr. Pitt?"

Mr. Pitt was furious. "What are you still doing in here? The foyer's finished! I told you to start cleaning the grounds—the governors will be arriving soon! The school has to look perfect!"

The foreman glowered at him.

"It might *look* finished, Mr. Pitt, but there are a number of safety issues that need attention. Most of the building work has been done too quickly, and if we don't fix it now—"

"There's no time for that!" Pitt snapped. "All of you outside, now!"

The foreman shared a look with the workers, and they stormed out. Mr. Pitt smiled. Even *he'd* been a little worried that the work wouldn't be completed in time, but he had to admit that the Pitt Building looked magnificent. He was one step closer toward the fruition of his grand plan. *Nothing* could ruin it now.

His cell phone rang.

Mr. Pitt looked at the screen, and frowned. It wasn't a number he recognized. "Hello?"

"*Er . . . hello!*"

The voice on the end of the line was high-pitched and wobbly. It sounded like somebody trying to hide an American accent.

"Who is this?" said Mr. Pitt.

"*My name?*" said the voice. "*Of course! I'll tell you my name right away! It's Mrs., er . . . Journalist.*"

Mr. Pitt raised an eyebrow. "Mrs. Journalist?"

"*No, that's not right,*" said the voice. "*Sorry. What I meant to say is that I am a journalist. A journalist called Mrs. . . . Max.*"

It sounded like someone in the background was getting pretty annoyed with Mrs. Max. "How can I help you, Mrs. Max?"

Mrs. Max cleared her throat. "*Well, Mr. Pitt, I have some excellent news for you. I'm from the magazine* Great Boarding Schools Monthly, *and we'd like to interview you for an article about what an inspirational headmaster you are!*"

Mr. Pitt gasped. "That's wonderful!"

"*We need to do the interview right away!*" said Mrs. Max. "*Our office is on the other side of town, so if you leave now it should take you only twenty minutes to—*"

"Can't we do the interview over the phone?" said Mr. Pitt.

There was a long pause.

"*That's a really good question,*" said Mrs. Max. "*Er . . . because . . .*"

"Is it because you need to take my photo as well?" suggested Mr. Pitt.

"*Yes! That's it!*" cried Mrs. Max with relief. "*We need your photo! Now, as I said, it's a twenty-minute drive from St. Goliath's, so—*"

Mr. Pitt was already running to his car. "I'll be there in ten!"

· · ·

Max and Sasha were crouched in the bushes outside their dorm window. Sasha put away his phone and tapped Max on the shoulder.

"Did it work? Is he leaving?"

Max followed Mr. Pitt's car through the microscope goggles. Even from this far away, he could still make out the look of delight on the headmaster's face as he sped through the gates.

"Yes! Let's go!"

The two boys shot from the bushes and into the sparkling new foyer of the Pitt Building. Sasha whistled.

"Wow! Look at that walkway! This place is *amazing*."

Max shrugged. "Mmph. *Looks* amazing, sure." He

pointed to a staircase. "See those screws? They're supposed to be lined up. A rush job! That could cause all kinds of problems later on. Mr. Darrow always used to say—"

"Sorry I asked," muttered Sasha.

They snuck down the corridor until they found the sports hall. All the equipment was piled in the middle of the room. Max rifled through it until he found what he was looking for: a fencing mask, a handful of skipping ropes and a big whiteboard and pen.

"There!" he said. "Now, let's take these to the boardinghouse and—"

Max froze. A man was striding across the sports hall toward them with a face like thunder—the foreman.

"You two! What are you doing?" he shouted. "This is a building site!"

Max panicked—they'd been caught red-handed. The foreman pulled his phone out of his pocket.

"I'm calling Da—I mean, *Mr. Pitt* right away! You, with the eye shadow and the earrings—what's your name?"

Max glowered. "They're not earrings! They're hearing aids, and . . ."

And that was when Max remembered that being severely deaf could sometimes be severely useful. He turned to the foreman and smiled.

"I CAN'T HEAR WHAT YOU'RE SAYING."

The foreman looked blank. "What?"

"I'M DEAF." Max pointed at his hearing aids. "I CAN'T UNDERSTAND WHEN YOU'RE SHOUTING AT ME LIKE THAT. IT'S ACTUALLY QUITE UPSETTING FOR ME, IF YOU MUST KNOW."

Sasha's eyes lit up. "That's right! Don't you know how insensitive it is to shout at someone with hearing problems? That's the sort of thing that can get you fired!"

The foreman panicked. "Hey, there's no need for that, I didn't realize—"

Sasha patted him on the back.

"Hey, don't beat yourself up about it. It's an easy mistake to make, isn't it? Anyone could do it!"

The foreman nodded gratefully. "That's right!"

Sasha smiled. "We'll just take what we need and go. I'll make sure Max doesn't make an official complaint against you. Sound good?"

The foreman looked relieved. "Yes! Thank you!"

"Don't mention it," said Sasha. "Have a good day."

The foreman practically skipped out of the room. It was the Sasha effect—five seconds with him and *anyone* was smiling.

"Now, *that*," said Max, "was teamwork."

"You were great!" said Sasha, giving him a high five.

Max grinned. "Let's go! We've got *just* enough time to save the floor people before Pitt gets back! Luke will have already spoken to the Reds and Greens by now—he'll be waiting for us."

Sasha looked worried. "How are we going to get into Mr. Darrow's room without Joy seeing us?"

"We'll climb the gutter outside his window and sneak in!" said Max. "Joy's waiting outside our dorm, remember? Once we're done, we can climb back through our window and she'll be none the wiser!"

Sasha gulped. "But . . . what if she gets into our dorm somehow and sees we're not there?"

Max rolled his eyes.

"She's five years old! What's she going to do—break down the door?"

• • •

Joy broke down the door.

It hadn't taken long for the Sparkle Pony Summer Club to find the large wooden statue of St. Goliath in the corridor. With all fifty girls holding it, and Joy riding it like a rodeo bull, the statue made an ideal battering ram. The door gave on the tenth try.

"Saaaaashaaaa!" Joy cried, leaping into the dorm. "No more hiding! Come out and play with—"

Joy looked round in shock. The room was empty and the window was open, curtains flapping in the breeze.

"They've gone!" she cried. "Quick—upstairs! Get them before . . ."

But the Sparkle Pony Summer Club weren't listening to her. They were staring at something on the floor, their mouths open and their eyes captivated.

"It's . . . it's here," one of them whispered.

It was a large cardboard box, hidden behind the curtains. Written on the side were the words:

CONFISCATED CANDY
KEEP OUT!

"Our sweets," said one of the girls. "I thought he'd thrown them all away!"

Joy tore off the lid and gazed inside. An entire summer's worth of forbidden sweets lay in the box: chocolates, jelly beans, gummy bears . . .

She held up a handful and smiled, letting the sweets pour through her fingers.

"Girls, change of plan. We're staying right here."

CHAPTER 23

"Whoa, Excelsior!"

"Miss Binkles."

Sigh. "Whoa, *Miss Binkles*."

Miss Binkles came to a gentle stop on top of the dune. Luke shielded his eyes and gazed up at the Sky Compass. They had been following it for twenty long minutes now, and it didn't seem to be getting any closer.

"Why are we stopping?" said Ivy.

"Mmph," said Luke. "I thought I heard something behind us. Guess it must have been—"

Ivy tackled him to the ground just as a warfly buzzed overhead. The two of them rolled into balls and hid beneath Miss Binkles, their hearts pounding, barely daring to breathe. The warfly hovered above them. Luke could see the fly rider on its back gazing down, wondering whether it was worth getting a closer look at the flea below. . . .

"Act natural, Miss Binkles," Luke whispered.

Miss Binkles did her best. The fly rider paused, then turned the warfly round and buzzed away.

Luke picked himself up.

"Whew! That was the closest one yet. Feels like we're seeing more and more of them now."

Ivy didn't answer. She was watching the warfly disappear across the desert with a faint smile.

"Amazing, aren't they? You could go *anywhere* on one of those—right up to the ceiling, even! Can you *imagine* what the Floor looks like from up there?" She looked at the ceiling longingly.

"What is it with you and flying?" said Luke. "You had all those drawings in your hut—flies, gnats, that one of you on a moth . . ."

Ivy looked shocked for a moment, but quickly regained her composure. She brushed the sand off herself.

"You wouldn't understand. I've been stuck under the Bed my whole life. We're not all kings, you know—we don't get whatever we want at the click of our fingers!"

Luke scowled. "I'm not a king! And I never *asked* to be one, you know!"

Ivy laughed. "Don't be so oblivious. You've been given more choices than most of us get in a lifetime!"

"I—"

Luke stopped—partly because he didn't know what *oblivious* meant but also because there was a spear jamming into his throat.

"Don't move," said a voice.

The spear was pointing straight out of the sand in front of him, but Luke couldn't see anyone holding it. He glanced at Ivy—sure enough, another spear was sticking out of the sand behind her and jamming into her back.

"Put down the club," said the voice. "And the sword."

Luke and Ivy dropped their weapons. There was a pause; then the dunes in front of them warped and shifted. They were suddenly surrounded by dozens of people in desert camouflage, their faces covered by hoods. The person in front of Luke held the spear steadily at his jugular.

"State your purpose—why are you here?"

Luke gulped. "We're ... we're searching for the Wise Man."

"And what is the magic word?"

Luke thought about it.

"Please?"

There was a pause. The sand person lowered the spear and removed the hood.

"Wow, right the first time," she said.

The woman standing in front of Luke had a shaved

head with fine blue across her scalp. The other sand people also removed their hoods. They *all* had shaved heads: some with red stubble, some green, some blue.

"Congratulations," said the woman, handing Luke his sword. "You passed the test. Now we can show you the way to the Holy Mountain."

Ivy was appalled. "That was a *test*?"

The woman nodded. "All those who wish to join the Wise Man must pass the test."

"Has anyone ever failed?"

The woman thought about it.

"No. Shall we?"

She hopped onto Miss Binkles and pulled Luke up beside her. A man with a shaved head appeared on a flea and grabbed Ivy, and they bounded across the desert side by side.

"You are closer to the Holy Mountain than you realize," the woman explained. "Most do not get so far—the Wise Man will be most impressed when he finds out, Prince Luke."

Luke was surprised. "You know who I am?"

The woman smiled. "I was a Blue once, but I left King Adam to follow a more important path. My name is Follower 43." She pointed to the man riding with Ivy. "That is Follower 18—he was once a powerful Green, but he, too, joined the Wise Man to find the answers to life's bigger questions: Why are we here? What is our purpose?"

"And what did the Wise Man say?" said Ivy.

Follower 18 turned round, tears in his eyes.

"'Stop asking me questions and leave me alone,'" he said reverently.

Luke and Ivy shared a glance.

"We're here!" said Follower 43. "The Holy Mountain!"

They were directly beneath the Sky Compass. The dunes rose slightly and then dipped into a deep valley, one so deep that the mountain inside was hidden from view. The mountain was made of rippling black folds piled on top of each other.

"People say that the Holy Mountain was once the clothing of the Great One himself," Follower 43 explained. "The Wise Man settled here after the tribes refused to reunite, and focused on trying to bring back the Great One."

Miss Binkles came to a stop before a deep cave in the Mountain's side.

"Behold!" said Follower 43. "The Pocket—the sanctuary of the Wise Man."

She led them inside. Luke was amazed—it was like a vast cathedral of black cloth, with walls stretching so high you couldn't see where they ended. Ahead of them stood an enormous structure, glimmering in the half-light. Luke had never seen anything like it. It towered above them, and was made entirely of glass.

"What *is* that?"

Follower 43 bowed her head.

"*That* is the Bottle which once held the Serum, the source of all life on the Floor. The Wise Man found it in the desert, and his followers dragged it here for him to study. He spent many weeks inside that bottle, gathering artifacts from all over the desert and working on them tirelessly. No one knows what he was building—he took everything with him when he left."

Luke strode toward the Bottle. "We need to speak to him right away! If we don't get back to the Red Kingdom before the Bin King attacks, then . . ."

He trailed off as Follower 43's words sank in.

"Did . . . did you just say he *left*?"

Follower 43 nodded. "About, ooh, I don't know . . . an hour ago, maybe."

Luke and Ivy stared at her in dismay. Follower 43 didn't seem to notice.

"Right after Demon first appeared through the Bedroom Door," she explained, "the Wise Man ran outside, looked at him and went into a trance. He often goes into trances, but this one was different. Nothing could wake him from it! But once Demon and his accomplice left, he came out of it again. He gazed at each of his beloved followers in turn, took a deep breath and said: 'We're stuffed.'"

"It was so moving," said Follower 18, wiping away another tear.

"Then he took his things and ran into the desert," said Follower 43. "We tried to follow him, but he told us to 'get lost.' We have spent the last sixty minutes in deep discussion of his words—get lost *where*? Get lost *how*? Is it possible to become lost by choice, or must one already be in a state of lostness?"

Luke didn't waste any time—he grabbed Ivy and started dragging her outside.

"We have to go, right now! If we don't find the Wise Man soon, then—"

BAM.

A huge boulder flew through the entrance to the Pocket and slammed into the wall beside them, missing them by fractions of a millimeter before rolling to a stop on the sand.

Luke's eyes goggled. Written on the side of the boulder, in bright-green paint, were the words

WE'RE OUTSIDE

"Oh crud," he whispered.

He stepped out of the Pocket, and his stomach dropped. The entire Green army surrounded the Holy Mountain. The sky was thick with warflies, all of their catapults aimed directly at Luke and Ivy.

And striding across the sand toward them was the Bin King.

CHAPTER 24

Luke could smell the Bin King from where he stood. He wore long flowing robes made from used tissues, and a crushed metal crown molded from scraps of a bottle cap. His long green hair was scraped into greasy curtains that hung on either side of his face.

"Well, well! If it isn't the cowardly traitor, Prince Luke of the Blues!"

Luke drew his sword and Ivy grabbed her club. Miss Binkles growled.

"Careful now!" laughed the Bin King. "You wouldn't want your *loyal subjects* to come to any harm, would you?"

He nodded to the soldiers behind him. They parted, revealing a handful of Blue prisoners kneeling in a circle of spears on the sand.

"One word from me and they're dead," said the Bin King. "So choose your next move *wisely*, Prince Luke."

Luke's eyes darted between the prisoners and the Bin King. His sword trembled in his grip.

"You . . . you have to listen to me," he said. "This is all a mistake. I never told Giant to attack your warfly!"

The Bin King looked surprised. "How odd—that's not what *I've* been told. . . ."

He nodded to the soldiers again, and they dragged Malcolm from the crowd of prisoners. His beard was torn and tattered, and he was still wearing just his underpants.

"I'm sorry, Luke!" Malcolm cried. "They made me tell them everything!"

"We found him wandering the desert," said the Bin King. "He really has been *most* helpful! Explaining all about your alliance with the one you call *Giant,* and your quest to turn the Reds against us. Of course, all that stuff about you trying to *sacrifice your people* was my own embellishment. I hope you don't mind. . . ."

Luke trembled with rage. "What do you want, Bin King?"

The Bin King smiled. "I should have thought that was *obvious,* Luke. I want to execute you in front of your people! After you've confessed to all your crimes, of course. Slaves are so much more servile when they realize their only hope is gone. With the Blues as a workforce, defeating the Reds will be easy!"

Ivy stepped forward. "Good luck—the Reds will *never* be your slaves!"

The Bin King nodded. "Oh, of course not. I'm not going to enslave the Reds—I'm going to kill them!"

Luke and Ivy gasped. The Bin King turned to face the desert.

"You see, there are things about the Floor that only I know. For example, the Bin is running out of food. There's only enough to keep the whole Floor going for a few more days, if we're lucky."

The soldiers stepped forward, their spears leveled. Luke, Ivy and Miss Binkles flung themselves against the walls of the mountain.

"So I figured it was time to make the kind of decision only a king can make," said the Bin King. "With the Reds gone, there'll be enough food to feed the Greens for weeks to come—*and* we'll have the Blues as our slaves! A perfect solution, don't you think?"

"You monster," sneered Ivy. "Don't you realize how pointless that is? Even without the Reds, the food's going to run out eventually!"

Luke stepped forward. "She's right, Bin King! We can work out another way, one for all the tribes to survive!"

The Bin King chuckled. "Perhaps, Luke. But you're forgetting something important—I've tasted power. *True* power. I took on Demon, and I won! Soon I'll rule the entire Floor, and the Great One himself will bow down to me! And the only thing that stands in my way is *you!*"

The soldiers grabbed Luke and Ivy. They thrashed and fought with all their might, and Miss Binkles even managed to kick a few soldiers to the ground, but they were quickly overpowered. The Bin King leaned close, enveloping them with his stink.

"*Confess,*" he said. "Tell your precious Blues it was *you* who summoned Demon! *You* who tried to sacrifice them! Tell them that *I* am the one true king, and to bow down before me—"

"Never," said Luke.

"We'd rather just die, to be honest," said Ivy.

The Bin King was impressed.

"Very noble! Unfortunately, I *really* do need you to confess before I kill you, otherwise it'll make things tricky later on." He turned to his soldiers. "Let's ramp things up a notch. Guards, cut off Malcolm's head!"

A soldier lifted Malcolm's head by the beard and raised his sword.

"*NO!*" Luke cried.

A horn blasted from the top of the dunes. Then another one sounded, and another, until the entire valley rang with a single note that vibrated in the air like sunshine. The executioner stopped midswing.

"It's the Red army!" cried Ivy.

The valley top around them glowed like fire. On every side stood thousands of Reds waving flags and shouting battle cries. A single figure descended into the valley on fleaback: a woman in a bright-red tunic, her hair braided into a razor-sharp plait that wound down one arm.

"The Red Queen!" said Ivy. "Luke, we're saved!"

The Red Queen leapt off her flea and faced off against the Bin King, her eyes burning with a fiery red.

"It's over, Bin King!" she announced, her voice hard as flint. "We have your army surrounded—your reign of terror ends here!"

The Bin King yawned. "Oh, does it? I'd have thought that my hundreds of warflies would easily overpower your mob of untrained savages. . . ."

"My savages include ten thousand archers," said the Red Queen. "All aiming their bows at your warflies."

She raised a hand, and the Red army lifted their arrows to the sky. Luke looked around with horror— the Holy Mountain was about to become the site of a massacre.

"Archers?" said the Bin King with interest. "You can't have had long to train them. If they miss, we'll slaughter every last one of you."

The Red Queen smirked. "*If* they miss."

The Bin King drew his sword. "So be it."

"Stop!"

Luke wrenched himself free from the guards and threw himself between the Bin King and the Red Queen. This was it—his one chance to save the Floor. He turned to the Red Queen.

"Your Majesty, I thank you for coming to the aid of the Blues in our time of need. But we cannot fight the Greens today! If we do, then *all* of us will die!"

He turned to the Reds on the valley top.

"I've learned a lot in the last hour. I've learned about the terrible things my father did to the Reds. And for that, I am truly sorry." He bowed his head. "I can never bring back the loved ones you've lost."

He clasped the Red Queen's hand and held it high.

"But today is our chance to start again, and make the Floor a better place for everyone! And we'll do it together! Together, we can choose peace over war! Together, we can live side by side and—"

The Red Queen snatched her hand away.

"Together? What are you talking about? I didn't come here to help the Blues—I came here to kill them, right after I've killed the Greens!"

Luke turned pale. "You what?"

The Red Queen turned to her army.

"The Reds have suffered long enough at the hands

of two monstrous kings—the age of the Red Floor begins now!"

The Red army bellowed. Ivy broke free and ran to the Red Queen.

"Your Majesty, no! Luke has a plan to reunite the tribes and fix everything and—"

"No," said the Red Queen. "Nothing can ever fix what's happened between us."

She raised one hand, and the Red archers pulled back their bows. The Green fly riders loaded their catapults and aimed them at the Red army. The guards surrounding the Blue prisoners stepped forward, the circle of spears growing tighter. . . .

And the valley filled with shadow.

Screams went up on every side. Reds and Greens alike dropped their weapons and pointed at the sky. Something was blocking the light from the Bulb, filling the air like a thundercloud—something enormous. And it was getting closer.

Luke looked up. It was Giant, but he had changed. He had no face.

And he was *flying.*

CHAPTER 25

"Lower!" said Max.

Sasha carefully loosened his grip on the rope.

"Just a little bit more . . . ," said Max.

Max was hanging from the ceiling fan by a skipping rope tied round his waist. Sasha stood on the bed, holding the other end so that Max—who was wearing a fencing mask—dangled above the floor like a pantomime angel.

"Stop!" said Max. "That's close enough. Don't forget, I'm still wearing the microscope goggles under this mask!"

Sasha gripped the rope. "Will you still be able to lip-read?"

Max nodded. "It won't be easy, though. So long as I can find Luke . . ."

Max gazed at the pile of old clothes beneath him. It looked like he and Sasha had arrived just in time—

hundreds of thousands of Reds, Greens and Blues stood on the sand, staring up in shock. He searched the crowds. . . .

"There!" said Max. "He's with another king and queen—he did it! He brought everyone together!"

"So what now?" Sasha asked.

Max smiled. "It's simple. Everything that's happened so far has been because of a misunderstanding. It's time to tell them the truth."

Sasha frowned. "You're going to do all that with *sign language*?"

"Of course not!" said Max.

He reached for the whiteboard he'd stuffed into the back of his trousers and took a marker from one pocket.

"I'm going to write to them. And *you*, Sasha, are going to help me work out what to say."

• • •

The Bin King leapt to attention and bellowed to the crowds around him.

"Behold, Prince Luke has summoned Demon! War-flies, attack!"

Before Luke could stop them, the warflies had turned to face Giant and fired their catapults. For a moment the air was thick with flying metal, a death cloud soaring toward Giant's face....

Which bounced right off him. The metal guard covering his face was like a force field—nothing could get through it.

The Bin King's face fell. There was an awkward silence.

"RUUUUUN!" screamed the Bin King.

He charged to the nearest warfly, shoved off the fly rider and buzzed away as fast as he could. The rest of the warflies quickly followed, and the Green army began to flee the valley.

"Quick!" Luke grabbed Ivy. "We have to get out of here!"

A hand stopped him—the Red Queen.

"So it's true. You *do* control Demon!" she cried. "Why else would he have turned up now, if not to protect you? Well, if it's a blood sacrifice he wants, then the Reds will give him one—a royal one! Guards, seize him!"

A dozen Red soldiers grabbed Luke and started dragging him away. Ivy leapt at them with rage, swinging her club, but it was no use. Luke looked up to the sky desperately.

"Giant, quick! Tell them you don't want to hurt anyone!"

But Giant wasn't even looking at him. Instead, he

was holding a huge white slab in his hands, and doing something very, *very* slowly to the back of it. . . .

"Execute him!" cried the Red Queen.

The soldiers threw Luke to the ground and held him down. Luke struggled to escape.

"For crying out loud, why aren't you listening? Giant's trying to help us! For Great One's sake, *let me go!*"

The soldiers let him go instantly.

"Oh," said Luke. "Thanks."

No one said anything. They were all staring up at the sky.

"Er . . . Luke," said Ivy, "you might want to see this."

Luke looked up, and his mouth fell open.

Giant had turned round the slab. There were words on it.

HI EVERYONE!
SORRY ABOUT THIS
***BIG** MISUNDERSTANDING*
I KILLED THE FLY, COMPLETE MISTAKE
DIDN'T MEAN TO
OOPS!!!

The crowd was stunned.

"Oops?" said the Red Queen.

There was a moment's pause, then Giant tur
board round and started writing again.

ACTUALLY IT WAS SASHA
BUT OUR FAULT ANYWAY
NOT LUKE'S
#SORRY

The crowd was dumbstruck.

"See?" said Luke smugly. "*Told* you I didn't d

"Who's *Sasha*?" said Ivy.

Luke looked around. Everyone was staring a

"What?"

"Go on, ask," said the Red Queen. "You're
who summoned him."

Luke glowered. "For the last time, I didn't s
him—"

"*You might want to pretend you did so she*
kill you," whispered Ivy.

Luke swallowed, and turned to the sky. He
sure to speak slowly and clearly.

"Er ... hi, Giant. Could you tell us who S
please?"

Giant wrote another message.

THE ONE ON THE BED

The crowd turned to the vast mountain on the horizon. Standing on the Bed was the second Giant, looming over the Floor like a towering angel of death.

He gave them a little wave.

"See?" said Luke. "They're not monsters!"

The valley was filling up again. Everyone seemed to have forgotten about the battle: Reds and Greens and Blues stood side by side, their eyes fixed on what was happening above them.

"But ... why are they here?" said someone. "What do they want?"

Hundreds of people were watching Luke now, waiting for him to speak. He cleared his throat.

"Er... why are you helping us, Giant?" he asked.

There was a long pause. Then ...

I'VE COME TO TAKE YOU ALL AWAY
TO SOMEWHERE ELSE
SOMEWHERE BETTER

A gasp of disbelief went up from the crowd.

"Take us away?"

"No! It can't be!"

"It's ..."

"*The Great One!*" Malcolm stumbled through the

crowd, his hands held up to the heavens. "He has re-turned to take us all to paradise!"

"Why is that man not wearing any clothes?" some-one muttered.

The effect of Malcolm's words on the crowd was electric. More and more people were gathering round them, arguing and panicking, not able to believe it could be true. Luke turned back to the sky.

"Giant, are you really the Great One?" he asked. "The one who created the Floor, and gave us life?"

This time, the wait was much longer. The crowd stood for many seconds, their breath held in antici-pation. Giant didn't move—it was like he was trying to work something out in his head.

And then, just when it looked like there was going to be no reply, he wrote on the slab and turned it around.

YEAH THAT'S ME

The crowd went wild.
"It's a miracle!"
"He has returned!"
"Praise be to the Great One!"
"How can we be sure it's him?"

Everyone stopped. Ivy was looking up at the sky, concerned.

"I mean, he just *says* he's the Great One, right?" she said. "He could be lying!"

The crowd grumbled. There seemed to be no way of proving whether Giant was their divine creator or a great big fibber.

"Ask if he knows where my keys are," said a Green.

Everyone turned to look at him. The Green shrugged.

"The Great One knows *everything*, right? So he'll know where my keys are."

Everyone agreed this made perfect sense.

"Oh, *come on*," said Luke. "You don't actually think—"

"Ask him or we'll break your legs," said the Red Queen, grabbing him by the scruff of the neck.

Luke groaned. "Giant, do you know where . . ."

"Keith," said the Green.

"Do you know where *Keith's* keys are?"

There was a long wait.

ARE THEY IN YOUR POCKET?

Keith reached into his pocket with a trembling hand . . . and pulled out the keys.

"It . . . *it is him!*" he cried. "*It's the Great One!*"

The crowd went ecstatic, holding one other and cry-

174

ing with joy. The valley was filled with people of every color now—Red and Green and Blue, arm in arm. Luke lifted his head in amazement.

"So, what do we do, Great One? Tell us!"

The writing appeared quickly this time.

GATHER THE WHOLE FLOOR TOGETHER
I'LL COME BACK FOR YOU
LEAVING LUKE IN CHARGE FOR NOW
BYE!
~~MA~~ THE GREAT ONE

The soldiers who had been trying to execute Luke only moments before fell to their knees.

"Your Majesty!" they begged. "Forgive us!"

"We didn't know!"

"Lead us, Prince Luke!"

Luke looked up. The eyes of the entire valley were on him now, waiting for his next words. It felt strange—it felt *good*, actually.

"Well ... you heard what the Great One said!" he announced. "Spread the word to every corner of the Floor—we're going to paradise!"

The tribes cheered. The Red Queen grabbed Luke's hand and held it high.

"All hail *King* Luke, voice of the Great One!"

"Luke! Luke!" the crowd chanted.

Luke gazed across the crowd, lapping up the adoration. There was a strange feeling in his chest, like it was inflating so much it might suddenly explode.

So this is what power feels like, thought Luke. *No wonder the Bin King likes it so much.*

Ivy looked nervously at the crowd.

"Luke, are you sure about this? I thought the whole point of being one tribe was to get rid of kings."

"What are you worrying about?" said Luke. "Look at them, Ivy!"

The people ahead were dancing together, hand in hand—Reds with Greens, and Greens with Blues.

"A moment ago, these people were all ready to kill each other. We didn't need the Wise Man after all. The Floor is reunited, and it's all thanks to me!"

Ivy frowned. "You mean all thanks to the Great One."

"Yeah, sure," said Luke, waving her away. "That's what I meant."

Ivy looked at him. "Luke, I have a really bad feeling about this. Something doesn't feel right . . . something's *weird. . . .*"

But Luke wasn't listening—all his attention was focused on the people chanting his name. Before Ivy had finished her sentence, he had left her and walked into the crowd with his arms outstretched. People started piling on top of each other to be the first to touch him.

"Luke, stop...."

He didn't stop—he didn't even hear her. Ivy watched as the crowd swallowed him up completely.

CHAPTER 26

Max swung down from the ceiling fan and landed on the bed, his heart pounding. He tore off the fencing mask and goggles.

"How did you know the keys were in his pocket?" said Sasha.

"Lucky guess," said Max. "And it worked—look at them!"

The people around the pile of clothes were celebrating—and that wasn't all. You could see others from all over the room heading toward the clothes, drawn by Max's message. The different colors were finally mixing—Red and Green and Blue, together as one.

"The Greens tried to attack, but the mask protected me!" said Max. "Now they've all made peace—the war's over!"

Sasha was reading the words on Max's whiteboard. " 'The Great One'? What does that mean?"

Max shrugged. "Oh, *that*. Slight confusion—they think I'm their god or something."

Sasha's eyes bugged out of his head. "Their *god*?!"

"I know—it's perfect!" said Max. "Now they'll finally do whatever we tell them!"

Sasha looked uncomfortable. "I thought you said we were going to be honest."

"I *am* being honest!" said Max. "We *are* going to take them away, aren't we? I can tell them the whole truth once we get them to paradise!"

"Paradise?"

"Well, almost," Max explained. "Come on, I'll show you!"

He leapt out the window and scrambled back down the gutter. It was all Sasha could do to keep up with Max as they ran through the bushes and into Mr. Darrow's vegetable patch.

"I can't believe we didn't think of it before—the potting shed!"

Max threw open the door and ran inside.

"It's perfect! It's big enough to fit all the people, it's warm and dry, and best of all, no one ever comes here! All it needs is a little clean."

Max swept his arm across the tables, sending tools and pots clattering to the floor. Sasha watched with concern. Max was breaking things and hadn't even noticed. Sasha tried waving his arms to get his attention, but Max didn't notice *that* either. He grabbed Max's arm.

"Max, are you sure about this? You said we had to do everything perfectly or it could go wrong. Don't you think *lying* to all those people—telling them you're their god—might be a mistake?"

Max shook his head. "We stopped them from fighting each other, and now we're giving them a place they can live in safety for the rest of their lives! Surely one lie has got to be worth all *that*?"

Sasha fumbled. "I . . . I suppose."

Max started collecting all the trays and lining them up on the tables.

"This is our final chance to save them. All we have to do is scoop the people into a couple of trays, bring them here and we're done! Mr. Darrow's world is safe, King Luke can protect the people for us and, best of all, Mr. Pitt will never find out!"

"You're sure?"

Max clapped a hand on Sasha's back.

"Sasha, I've never been more certain of anything in my life."

• • •

Mr. Pitt stood at the entrance to the Pitt Building.

"My—my school."

The freshly painted foyer walls were covered in crayon smears. The beautiful X-shaped walkway was strewn with lost-and-found items. Someone had set off all the fire extinguishers.

The Pitt Building had been sabotaged.

The foreman had called Mr. Pitt when he was halfway to town, garbling something about the school being under attack. Mr. Pitt had turned the car round and sped back as fast as he could, but he was already too late. The grounds were covered in library books, footballs and Hula-Hoops. It was like a bomb had gone off.

Whoever had done it had worked fast, and in a group.

"Uuuurrrrrugh."

Mr. Pitt shrieked and leapt backward, into an ornamental fern. The groan had come from a pile of rags on the reception desk. Mr. Pitt prodded the pile. It groaned again.

"Who's in there?" he cried. "Show yourself!"

The pile of rags was a five-year-old girl wearing every costume from the drama department. Her eyes were dazed and swollen and her mouth stained green. On her front was a badge that said 5 TODAY.

"Candy," Joy moaned. "So much candy . . ."

"Mr. Pitt!"

He spun round. The foreman was standing at the door, his eyes wide with panic. *"Come quick!"*

Mr. Pitt wedged Joy under one arm like a rugby ball and followed the foreman outside. The grounds were in chaos. The school's annual supply of toilet paper was wrapped round every tree in sight, and the builders were chasing the rest of the Sparkle Pony Summer Club across the playing fields. The girls were in a sugar-induced frenzy. They'd raided the power tools locker and were brandishing drills and sanders, gibbering in tongues.

Mr. Pitt was speechless. The governors would be here in a matter of hours. He held Joy at arm's length like a bad dog and shook her.

"How—how did this happen? *Where are Max and Sasha?!"*

Joy pointed with a shaking hand. "Boardinghouse . . . top floor . . ."

Mr. Pitt looked up. There, clambering down the side of the boardinghouse and running into the bushes, were Max and Sasha. He looked at the window they'd just climbed out of. Mr. Darrow's bedroom.

The veins on his forehead pinged like buttons bursting on a shirt.

"DARROOOOW!"

Of course—it all made sense now. Pitt had foolishly

thought he was rid of Mr. Darrow. The man had been a thorn in his side ever since he came to St. Goliath's . . . and now Max and Sasha were trying to continue his legacy, right under his nose! *That* was why Max had returned to school so early—so he could humiliate Mr. Pitt in front of the governors! So he could destroy his plans for greatness at the last second!

Mr. Pitt knew *exactly* what he had to do now. He should have done it when he first had the chance. Stamp out every scrap of Mr. Darrow's memory, once and for all.

Mr. Pitt turned to the boardinghouse, and ran.

CHAPTER 27

King Luke sat on his throne, gazing over the sea of Red, Blue and Green. The entire Floor was camped in the desert ahead of him—millions of them. It was beautiful... and it was all because of him.

"Your Majesty?"

Malcolm stood beside him on the wooden platform, back in his rightful place as king's advisor, and thankfully wearing clothes.

"The girl wishes to talk to you."

"Girl?"

"The angry one, Your Highness."

Luke nodded. "Ah, Ivy! Send her up."

There weren't many people who were allowed onto King Luke's special platform—he had insisted it be that way since everyone had started bothering him with questions for the Great One. *When will my children get married, should I invest in a new house, do trousers suit me better than shorts* ... they just kept coming. At first Luke had refused to accept any questions, but when people started offering him gifts to do so, he was hardly going to object, was he?

Ivy stormed up the steps, shoving Malcolm out of the way.

"What the *hell* are you doing?" she demanded.

Luke was surprised. "What do you mean?"

Ivy held out her arms.

"The special platform you made people build for you? The gifts? The throne? Making Miss Binkles an *advisor*?"

She pointed at Miss Binkles, who was curled up on a plush gold cushion beside the throne and wearing a small crown.

"Ivy, be reasonable!" said Luke. "People need *someone* in charge until the Great One comes back. The Red Queen's gathering the rest of the Floor and the Bin King ran away, so that leaves me. And I'm the one who reunited the tribes, aren't I?"

Ivy laughed bitterly. "Do they *look* reunited to you, Luke?"

She pointed to the sea of tents stretching out ahead of them. It was true—when people had first started gathering in preparation for the Great One's return, all the tribes had mixed together. But slowly, as more and more people arrived from across the Floor, they'd started forming separate camps. You could see the boundaries between them now—three huge expanses of Red, Green and Blue.

"People *still* don't trust each other!" said Ivy. "Fights are breaking out along the camp borders, and you're doing nothing to stop them!"

Luke rolled his eyes.

"People need time to become comfortable with each other, Ivy. One hour ago, you'd *never* have seen a Blue and a Green camped within even an inch of each other! That's progress."

He sat back down on his throne.

"Besides, I've already organized a police force to stop the fights at the borders—"

"You did," said Ivy angrily. "And they're all Blues."

Luke blinked. "Well, of course. I can *trust* them."

Ivy was shocked.

"Luke, what's happened to you? You told me you wanted a world without rulers. Now it's like you've forgotten what your quest was! You've turned into—"

"The Bin King, Your Majesty."

Luke and Ivy spun round. Malcolm was pointing behind them.

"He has returned."

A squadron of warflies droned through the air toward them, trembling the tents with the flapping of their wings. Luke could see the Bin King at the front, sheepishly waving a white flag. His warfly lowered to the platform, and he stepped off, along with a handful of fly riders. Miss Binkles growled at him.

"So!" said Luke. "You've finally come crawling back. What do you want, Bin King?"

The Bin King looked mortified. "Er . . . can we do this somewhere private, please?"

Luke shook his head. "Anything you have to say, you can say in front of the Floor."

By now thousands of people had stepped out of their tents to watch. Reds, Greens and Blues alike were staring at the Bin King with hate. He gulped.

"I wanted to . . . *apologize*, King Luke. For everything I've done."

Luke raised an eyebrow. "Like trying to kill me? Twice?"

"Er . . . yeah, like that," said the Bin King.

Luke said nothing. The crowds waited. You could have heard a pin drop. The Bin King cleared his throat nervously.

"We—that is, my fly riders and I—would like to join you. We'd like to come to paradise, please."

Luke raised an eyebrow. "Ask nicely."

The Bin King bowed. "Your Majesty, may we—"

"No, on your knees," said Luke. "I want to see you grovel."

Ivy was horrified. *"Luke!"*

The Bin King glared at him with fury. He got slowly to his knees, like it pained him, and spoke through gritted teeth.

"*Please*, Your Majesty. Please let us come with you."

Luke smiled.

"No."

The crowd gasped. The Bin King turned white. Luke drew himself up to his full height.

"There's no place for tyrants like you in paradise!" He pointed across the desert. "You and your fly riders are banished—forever! You wanted the whole Floor for yourself . . . well, now you can have it!"

The Bin King leapt to his feet. "You can't do that! I—"

But the crowds were already shouting him down— Reds, Greens and Blues, together as one.

"See?" said Luke. "Not even your own people want you, Bin King! Leave and never come back!"

The Bin King gave Luke a look of black loathing, then climbed back onto the warfly and flew off while the crowds booed him. Ivy watched, shaking her head in disbelief.

"Luke, the Great One told you to gather *everyone* together! You can't turn people away!"

Luke snorted. "The Bin King's a *monster*, not a person. He's the one who let your parents die!"

"And what about his fly riders?" said Ivy.

Luke was suddenly angry. "I'm trying to be a king, Ivy! That means making tough decisions sometimes!"

Ivy didn't answer him. She just stood gazing at him with a terrible sadness in her eyes.

"Oh, Luke."

The world turned black.

The Bedroom Door was opening. A shadow was passing across the Floor, covering them all in darkness. Luke turned from Ivy and waved to the crowds.

"The Great One has returned!"

A huge cheer went up from the Floor. Millions raced out of their tents to see the Great One for themselves. Adults waved flags, and children jumped up and down in excitement.

"Welcome back, Great One!" Luke cried. "We're ready to go!"

But the Great One said nothing. He just stood there. Whole seconds passed in silence. Luke shuffled his feet nervously and tried again.

"Tell us, Great One, what do we . . ."

The Great One lifted a foot and slowly stepped

forward. Luke sighed with relief—for a moment, it had looked a little embarrassing.

"He's coming—get ready, everyone! And don't be afraid: the Great One may look frightening, but—"

"Luke," said Ivy, "he looks different."

Ivy was right. The Great One was somehow taller now, and broader. The shadow he cast was longer. It was impossible to make out his face. Miss Binkles whined and hid under her cushion. Ivy stepped back.

"What's that in his hand?"

The Great One was holding something that looked like a long black sword, pointed down toward them.

"It . . . must be what he's going to take us to paradise in," said Luke uncertainly.

The Great One's feet came booming to a stop in front of them—so close it almost crushed some of the tents. The crowds jumped back in surprise. Even the feet were different—these weren't white trainers. They were black leather shoes instead.

The Great One held the black sword over the floor. Luke could see that it was a long tube, and inside was pure darkness. It hovered above their heads like a dying sun.

And suddenly Luke realized why the Great One looked so different.

"It's not the Great One! It's De—"

The world split in two.

Luke clutched his head in agony. The tube was making a noise like a thousand chain saws grinding against each other. He had thought that the Great One's voice was the loudest thing he had ever heard, but this was so much worse. It was like the sound was eating the desert. It was like the end of the world.

Luke spun round in terror. A whirlwind was forming on the sand around them, whipping the tents into a frenzy and scattering them like confetti. The black hole was dragging everything up from the ground, sucking it toward the darkness inside. . . .

"Everyone, run for your lives!"

But there was nowhere to run—the entire desert was being swallowed up. People were fleeing, trying to escape, but the force of the hurricane was too great. Luke watched in horror as his loyal subjects were picked off the ground in the hundreds and sucked into the black hole above them, screaming and spinning in terror. He grabbed Ivy and Miss Binkles.

"We have to get out of here, now! Or—"

Suddenly all the breath was drawn out of Luke's body, and the wooden platform cracked and split beneath them. He was trapped in the hurricane just like everyone else, tumbling up and up. Ivy disappeared from his grip, and Luke was alone, spinning closer and closer toward the darkness....

Luke looked up at Demon's face just before he was swallowed completely. Demon was smiling. But it wasn't the smile of a boy—it was the grimace of a man.

And then there was nothing.

CHAPTER 28

"There!"

Max surveyed the potting shed. It was finally finished—all the surfaces had been cleared and then filled with rows of carefully connected seedling trays. It wasn't exactly paradise, but it would do for now.

"You know what, Max?" said Sasha. "This is actually pretty nice!"

Max nodded. "And finished just in time. Come on!"

They each grabbed a tray and set off through the bushes.

"Mr. Pitt will be heading back to school," said Max breathlessly. "All we have to do is grab the floor people and—"

Max stopped. He hadn't noticed the school earlier when he was running from Mr. Darrow's room. But now he could see that the trees were covered in toilet paper.

There was paint everywhere. The playing fields looked much more glittery than Max remembered.

"Max, what's going on?" Sasha was panicking.

"I—I don't know!" Max said. "Unless—"

"*Joy!*"

She was leaning weakly against a tree in front of the boardinghouse, her mouth still stained green and oozing jelly beans. Sasha grabbed her.

"Joy, are you OK? What happened?"

She groaned. "We got into your dorm ... the candy ... Then I don't remember *anything*. ..."

Max looked over the devastation. Suddenly it all became clear.

"Quick! We have to get upstairs, before Mr. Pitt gets back and—"

"Too late," Joy murmured. "He went looking for you on the staff corridor. He just came back downstairs with a full trash bag and—"

Max's whole body flooded with horror.

"*NO!*"

He dropped the tray and ran into the boardinghouse as fast as he could, flying up the stairs and into the staff corridor. ...

He was too late. Mr. Darrow's door was wide open.

The bedroom was empty.

There wasn't a speck of sand on the floor. Every single model had been swept from the shelves. The bin, the pile of clothes, the castle, the microscope goggles . . . It was all gone. The only thing left was a vacuum cleaner, its long black nozzle pointing at the doorway like a sword.

Max felt a tap on his shoulder. It was the foreman.

"Oh, it's you!" said the foreman. "Er . . . you haven't seen Damon, have you?"

Max's blood froze.

"Damon?"

"I suppose you boys call him Mr. Pitt."

"Right here, Foreman."

Mr. Pitt emerged from the staircase, his eyes gleaming with triumph.

"Damon!" said the foreman. "Where have you *been*? The school's a complete disaster—there's no way it'll be ready in time for the governors! You have to call them and explain what happened, or—"

Mr. Pitt shook his head. "No, Foreman. The governors are expecting a finished school, and they're going to get one. Get your team and start cleaning."

The foreman gawped. "But we'll never—"

"Just do it," said Mr. Pitt, waving him quiet. "I'm afraid Max and I have some talking to do." He smiled. "Don't we, Max?"

Max wasn't looking at the headmaster anymore. He

was gazing at the empty bedroom, his eyes filling with tears. On the bed lay the whiteboard, still scrawled with the final message.

~~MA~~ THE GREAT ONE

"Oh, Luke," he whispered. "What have I done?"

CHAPTER 29

"Help! Help!"

The world lay scattered, and all was in darkness.

"Where are we?"

"Save us, Great One!"

Luke had never known darkness like this before. It was like drowning in a sea of black. It made no difference whether your eyes were open or closed, or whether you were up or down.

The only thing that proved you were alive was the screaming.

"Help! Somebody help us, please!"

Luke groped in the darkness. He was lying on the ground—he could feel sand beneath him. On every side, people were running and pushing and stumbling.

"Where are you, Great One?"

"Help us, Great One, please!"

"He's not listening."

The screams died, one by one. There was another noise cutting above them—a buzz that filled the darkness.

"Don't you get it?" said the voice. "The Great One was *never* coming! It was a trick, and you all fell for it!"

The buzz grew louder, closer.

"Funny, isn't it? You think it's all over . . . but it's only the beginning."

Lights were beginning to appear overhead. They were inside a vast black dome, the roof towering high above. They were surrounded by the shattered remnants of their world: cities and streets and houses, a million lives heaped into junkyard piles. The entire Floor stood huddled in fear in the center of the sand.

"Do you know what this place is?" said the voice. "It's called a 'Trash Bag.' You Reds and Blues may find it hard to see, but not us Greens. We've lived in darkness all our lives. You know, for a while I was even ashamed of it! Ha!"

The air was filled with warflies. The fly riders were holding torches, but instead of fire at the end, the torches glowed with a sickly green murk that illuminated the ground.

"But *now* I understand. It made us strong. It was preparing us . . . for this."

Ahead of them stood an enormous whale, its mouth stretched open like it was about to swallow them whole. Standing on its tongue was the Bin King.

"Let's pick up where we left off, shall we?"

The warflies came crashing onto the sand, and everyone screamed. People tried to run away, but it was no use—the soldiers were the only ones who still had weapons. The Bin King stepped forward, his mad eyes glinting.

"The age of the Green Floor has begun! From now on, the Reds and Blues are our slaves! Anyone who *dares* to disagree will be executed—and that goes for the Greens, too!"

The warflies began separating everyone into different colors, pushing and shoving and tearing groups apart. It was chaos—every time someone tried to fight back, they were shoved to the ground, or the fly riders picked them out with their whips—

"Stop!"

Luke fought to the front of the crowd.

"You can't do this, Bin King! The people won't let you win so easily!"

The Bin King watched him with mild amusement, then turned to the crowd.

"Behold: *King Luke of the Blues!* Who do you think

was working with Demon all along to trick us?" He pointed at Luke. "The darkness, the fear, the misery— this is all *his* fault!"

Luke shook his head. "They won't believe you anymore, Bin King—they know what you are!"

The Bin King laughed.

"Oh, poor, poor Luke. You really don't get it, do you?"

Luke cried out. Hands were grabbing him from every side.

"It doesn't *matter* if they believe me. The old world is gone. *I'm* in charge now."

The crowd stood and watched in silence as Luke was carried away by guards. The Bin King was right—no one was fighting back.

"And whoever rules in the darkness rules *everything*."

Luke struggled hopelessly. "No, please! You have to stop him!"

But it was no use. No one helped—no one moved. They just stood and watched. In the darkness, you couldn't tell who had red hair, or green hair, or blue hair. You couldn't tell which tribe was which anymore.

Everyone was equal. All you could see was fear.

CHAPTER 30

"Recognize this?"

Mr. Pitt placed the tiny model castle on the desk in front of Max and Sasha. They were in his brand-new office, which had big panes of glass overlooking the school grounds. You could see the builders outside, scrubbing puddles of PVA glue off the grass.

"I found it on Mr. Darrow's desk. Know what it says on the bottom?" He held up the castle. "'Mr. Darrow, I understand, Max.' Shall I read it again?"

Max stared back at him—he didn't even blink. Mr. Pitt put the castle back down.

"Oh, Max . . . where do I start? Breaking into a staff room, filling it with sand—that's two reasons for expulsion right there! And that's *before* I get to all the damage those girls caused to the school under your supervision. . . ."

Sasha stood up. "Sir, that was as much my fault as it was Max's and—"

"*Sit down, Sasha!*" Mr. Pitt barked.

Sasha sank back into his chair. Mr. Pitt smiled.

"The thing is, Max—I *know* it was Sasha's fault as well. I could say that the girls were to blame, too. I could even say that it was *my* fault for leaving fifty young girls under the care of two ten-year-old boys, ha ha! But I'm not going to do that. And do you know *why,* Max?"

Mr. Pitt leaned forward, until it seemed like his face was only inches from Max's.

"Because I believe in what's known as *getting rid of the rot.* Because if St. Goliath's is ever going to be the best school in the country—which it will—then we want the smartest children. The best athletes. The richest parents. We have plenty of room for people like Sasha . . . but none for people like you or Mr. Darrow. Not anymore."

Sasha stood back up. "Sir, this is outrageous! Max hasn't done anything wrong! You can't expel him just because—"

Mr. Pitt lifted the phone. "It'd be very easy to expel you, too, Sasha! I could call your parents right now and tell them Mr. Darrow's room was so filthy when I turned up, the floor was infested with *bugs*! I could write you a permanent record so vile, so *disgusting,* that no school will ever take you!"

Sasha looked at the phone, his eyes widening.

"Your choice. The question is . . . *is Max worth it?*"

Max waited for Sasha to answer—but he didn't. He was looking at Max helplessly, his face torn.

"Sasha?" said Max.

Sasha looked away, then quietly sat down. Mr. Pitt laughed.

"Excellent choice, Sasha! Why lose your place at St. Goliath's for someone like Max? By tomorrow, he'll be a distant memory, just like Mr. Darrow!"

Max stared at Sasha in disbelief, but Sasha wasn't looking at him anymore. He was staring at the floor, his face burning red under the hood of his onesie.

Mr. Pitt took a deep, satisfied breath.

"Soon, the last traces of Mr. Darrow will be gone. I've already cleared that old bedroom, and every inch of it is sitting in the bins, waiting to be destroyed. I tell you, it's not been easy making St. Goliath's perfect—the Pitt Building's cost so much that there's no money left to pay the builders! But I'm not worried about small details like that. By the time anyone works out that the school is bankrupt, I'll be long gone. And Sasha will never breathe a word of this to anyone, will you, Sasha?"

Sasha kept staring at the floor.

A buzzer rang on Pitt's desk.

"Aha!" said Mr. Pitt cheerily. "That'll be the governors, waiting for me at the school gates! And just in time, too—looks like the builders have finished cleaning the grounds. You two can wait here until I'm done." He strode toward the door. "Oh, and here you go, boys—something to remember Mr. Darrow by."

He placed the model castle on the desk. Max reached out to take it—

SMASH

Mr. Pitt crushed the castle to splinters with his fist.

"I always win, Max. Never forget that."

He stepped out the door and locked it behind him.

Max stared at the shattered castle. The last remnant of the model world—gone. He had done everything he could to help Mr. Darrow, and he had failed.

Worse than that, he had failed Luke. He had failed *millions* of tiny people. They had all been relying on him . . . and now they were gone.

He felt a hand on his shoulder—Sasha was trying to talk to him.

"Max, listen—"

He shoved the hand off.

"You don't have to say anything, Sasha—I get it. We were never really friends, were we?"

Sasha looked surprised, but Max simply turned his chair away.

"It's fine—I understand. You go your way, and I'll go mine."

Max closed his eyes and waited for the old silence to settle over them once again. The one that had always signaled the end of their conversations in the past . . .

But the silence didn't come. Sasha swung his chair back round.

"How can you say that? How can you say we're not friends?" he cried.

Max was shocked by how hurt Sasha looked. "But—"

"I told you, Max—when I say I'm friends with someone, I *mean* it!"

He grabbed Max's index finger and crossed his own over it. *X.*

"*Friends,* remember?"

Max was confused. "But . . . you just sold me out to Mr. Pitt!"

Sasha rolled his eyes. "Are you kidding? I'd *never* sell you out to that idiot—I was buying us time!"

He heaved Max out of his chair.

"Didn't you hear what he said? He said Mr. Darrow's room was filled with *bugs*. He was talking about the tiny people! He was standing right in front of the greatest invention in the history of mankind, and he didn't have a clue! Which means they'll be in the bins—they're still alive! We can still save them!"

Max's face fell. "But how? Pitt's locked us in here and—"

The door burst open in a shower of wood. Max yelped and flew behind a chair.

"Hi, guys," said Joy.

She rode astride the wooden statue of St. Goliath, which was held aloft by the Sparkle Pony Summer Club. The girls all looked the worse for wear after their sugar bender, but apart from a few who twitched beneath foil blankets, they were ready for action.

"Joy! Girls!" said Max in disbelief. "What are you doing here?"

Joy jumped off the statue. "We've come to get you and Sasha out of here—and help you save the floor people!"

Max's eyes boggled. "You know about the floor people?"

Joy twisted one foot into the carpet.

"After you ran into the boardinghouse, Sasha told me everything—about Mr. Darrow's room, and Luke, and what the two of you had been up to. I'd *never* have done what I did if I'd known! So Sasha and I came up with a plan to trick Pitt and save the tiny world!"

"She knows where he took the trash bag, Max," said Sasha. "Let's go!"

He tried to drag Max out of the room, but Max pulled back.

"No, I can't let you do this. Don't you realize how much trouble you're in? You've just broken down Pitt's office door—you'll all be expelled!" He stepped away from the others. "You still have a chance. Let me go save the floor people on my own. I'll take responsibility for everything."

Sasha shook his head. "Max, we're doing this together."

"But—"

"No!" Sasha grabbed him again. "You're the best friend I've had since I got here. You're the one who showed me that small things matter. To never hurt a fly. I didn't know about *any* of that before I met you, Max— if you're doing this, then so am I!"

Joy grabbed their hands. "Me too."

Max looked at Sasha and Joy. They really didn't care about getting expelled.

"OK," said Max. "But we don't have long—Mr. Pitt's with the governors right now, and if they see us . . ."

Max trailed off. Sasha, Joy and the Sparkle Pony Summer Club were all smiling at each other.

"Yeah," said Sasha, "about that . . ."

• • •

Mr. Pitt strolled toward the school gates, whistling a merry tune. Everything was going just as he planned— the school was finished, Max was on his way out, the governors were waiting at the gates to congratulate him. . . .

Mr. Pitt stopped. There was only one governor at the gate. And the longer Mr. Pitt looked, the more the governor looked like three five-year-old girls wearing a long coat and sitting on each other's shoulders.

"Oi, you!" Pitt shouted.

The three girls leapt off each other and sprinted in different directions. Mr. Pitt chased the slowest and weakest one.

"Come back here!" he bellowed. "When I catch you I'll—"

He turned a corner and skidded to a stop. Standing in his path was the foreman, along with the rest of the builders. They looked furious.

"What's this about us not being paid?" said the foreman.

Mr. Pitt's face fell. "Er . . . pardon?"

"I just got off the phone with a journalist called Mrs. Max," said the foreman. "She's doing an exposé on the school and how there's no money left to pay us!"

The builders stepped forward, cracking their knuckles and wielding their sandwich tins and thermos flasks menacingly. Mr. Pitt backed away.

"That . . . that's not true! There's plenty of money! Now catch those girls, before—"

"No, Damon," said the foreman. "We've taken enough instructions from you, haven't we, lads?"

The builders grabbed Mr. Pitt and started dragging him backward. Mr. Pitt struggled feebly.

"Let go! Get your hands off me!"

Just before he was dragged behind the cricket sheds and pummeled mercilessly with sandwich tins and thermos flasks, Mr. Pitt looked up to the windows of his brand-new office. He could just make out Max and Sasha, standing beside the Sparkle Pony Summer Club.

They were all waving at him.

CHAPTER 31

Luke sat in prison, waiting for death.

He knew he wouldn't have to wait long. The Bin King had ordered every person in the trash bag to search for the Red Queen. After they found her, she and Luke would be executed in front of the whole Floor.

Luke wasn't afraid of death anymore—it was all he deserved.

He looked around his prison. He was inside the great curved belly of the whale. It was cavernous and dark, lit only by a single murky green torch. There was no way out except through the whale's mouth—and within the mouth were ten guards.

Luke laughed bitterly. As if he'd try to escape now—where would he go? Who would want to help him, after he'd doomed everyone to a lifetime of slavery and darkness?

Luke's heart stung. Not *Ivy*, that's for certain. She'd

been right all along. Luke had been given more choices than most people were given in their lifetimes, and every choice he had made had been wrong.

Luke had always thought he was lonely. *Now* he knew what true loneliness was.

The door at the end of the stomach opened. The guards had finally come for him.

"I'm ready." Luke stood up. "Let's just get it over with."

No reply. Footsteps came toward him in the gloom.

"You could try to sound a bit more excited about it," said a voice.

Luke frowned. The man in front of him was barely visible in the dim green light. He didn't look like the other guards. He was much older, for one thing. And there was something...odd about him. Something Luke couldn't put his finger on.

"Who are you?" said Luke.

The man didn't answer. He studied Luke from head to toe.

"Mmm. They were right. You *do* look like your father."

The man turned away and started wandering around the whale's stomach, running his hand along the walls and muttering under his breath. Luke was baffled.

"You knew my father?"

The man laughed. "I knew all the rulers, back in the beginning. He was a smart bloke, your dad... before he found that castle, at least. Then he turned into a right berk. Power does that to most people—even happened to you, from what I hear!"

The man sighed, and turned back to Luke.

"Still, you did a pretty good job before you doomed us for all eternity and so on. Besides, it's not the mistakes you make that matter, eh? It's how you fix them."

Luke finally realized what was so odd about the man. His hair had no color—it was completely white.

"Are you... the Wise Man?" he asked.

The man thought about it.

"Some people call me that," he said. "But you can call me Mr. Darrow."

CHAPTER 32

Max and Sasha ran down the stairs as fast as they could.

"Are you sure the builders will be able to stop Pitt?" asked Max.

"Of course!" said Sasha. "And even if they don't, the girls have moved on to plan B, remember? All we have to do is find that trash bag!"

They followed Joy's directions until they reached the basement of the Pitt Building. At the end was a single door, labeled WASTE DISPOSAL.

"That's it!" said Sasha. "We just need to find the bag in there and—"

They threw open the door . . . and stopped. The room was filled from floor to ceiling with black trash bags piled up in great tumbling heaps. It hadn't been emptied for weeks.

"Which bag is it?" said Max, looking around frantically.

Sasha shook his head. "I—I don't know! But it's got to be one of them . . . right?"

Max stared out across the sea of bags. There was no way of knowing which was the correct one. And even if they *did* find the right bag in time, what if they were already too late?

"Oh, Luke," Max whispered, "where *are* you?"

CHAPTER 33

Luke and Mr. Darrow walked out of the whale's stomach. Ahead of them, the throat stretched into darkness.

"Let's go!" said Mr. Darrow. "We haven't got much time!"

He started walking away, then stopped. Luke was standing at the entrance to the whale's stomach, staring at him.

"Aren't you going to explain *any* of this to me? Who you are? What you're doing here? Why you're helping me escape? The Great One? Demon?" He paused. "You know—*everything*?"

Mr. Darrow groaned. "Fine. Mind if we walk and talk? We've got a lot to do."

"Yes!" Luke leapt forward, and the two of them set off, up the whale's esophagus.

"So, let's start from the beginning," said Mr. Darrow. "I made the world, and—"

"Wait—you're the Great One?" said Luke.

"Yeah, yeah," said Mr. Darrow. "But don't go telling everyone. I've been trying to keep it quiet. You see, I never *meant* to create the Floor. It was all an accident!"

He kept walking.

"I've been a modeler all my life—and my greatest dream was to build a *living model.* Nothing fancy: just a little paradise with palm trees, lagoons, a few people, that kind of thing. Something to look after. See, an old man like me, with no family, no kids, you get lonely. And when I heard about this special serum that creates life, I was hooked! One drop, add some light and water, and presto! Tiny, living people! Cool, eh?"

Luke was completely lost. "Er . . . sure."

"A lot of people said it didn't really exist," said Mr. Darrow. "But I *knew* that the serum would be out there somewhere. All I needed to do was look properly. And I'm *good* at looking properly. Finally, after twenty years of searching, I found it—hidden away in the basement of an old abandoned museum in Massachusetts! Can you believe it?"

"What's a year?" said Luke. "What's a museum? What's Massachusetts?"

Mr. Darrow blinked.

"Er . . . none of that's important. What matters is that I found the serum. Finally, after five years of building the perfect sandbox paradise, I was ready to add the serum and create a living world!"

He blushed.

"But then I, er . . . gaffed it all up. I was about to add the serum, and the light in my room switched itself off. I got up to fix it and tripped over a bin in the darkness! I knocked the sandbox paradise to the floor, spilled half the serum on that, and the other half on me. Suddenly I'm shrinking to microscopic size, right in front of my own eyes! Turns out if you get any on your skin, you become tiny too. Who knew?"

Luke still had absolutely no idea what Mr. Darrow was talking about.

"I was pretty hacked off, let me tell you! Looked like I was going to be stuck on the floor forever. My only hope was that Max would arrive. I'd always told him to come to my room if I ever disappeared, so if something went wrong he'd be able to—"

"Max?"

"That giant boy you've been talking to this whole time. My apprentice. He's done a great job, that lad; I'm proud of him." Mr. Darrow frowned. "Don't know who the other kid is, though. I'm pretty certain he's the one who's been stealing my carrots."

"Sorry—what are carrots?" said Luke.

"Anyway," said Mr. Darrow, ignoring him, "Max turned

up, just like I'd predicted, but he didn't see me shouting at him on the floor. Then when he went, he left the bedroom light on . . . so the serum came to life! All it needs to work is light and water, and the sand was still wet from the tiny lagoon, remember? So the sand spread across the entire floor, thousands of people turned up out of nowhere, and that's how the Floor was made! Funny story, eh?"

They had reached the start of the whale's throat. Mr. Darrow glanced over the top of its enormous tongue.

"Humph—looks like the guards are still there," he muttered. "Never mind. We'll go out the blowhole."

He pointed up. Far above them was a tiny opening—a pinprick glimmer in the darkness. Luke could just make out a long rope dangling down from the opening to the throat. Mr. Darrow chuckled.

"And to think—I thought joining up the blowhole and the stomach was a mistake! Still, you live and learn."

He grabbed the rope and started climbing nimbly up the sides of the whale's throat.

"But hang on, you're the Wise Man," said Luke, following him. "You told everyone that the *Great One* made the world!"

Mr. Darrow shrugged. "Well, yeah—I knew no one would listen to me if I told the truth. So I sort of made up a story instead. I *had* to find a way of bringing Max back—he was the only one who'd be able to help me return to normal size before Damon came along and—"

"Damon? Don't you mean *Demon*?" said Luke.

"I mean *Damon*!" said Mr. Darrow. "See? That moron Malcolm wrote down everything wrong in that stupid Book of the Floor!"

Luke gawped. "*Malcolm* wrote the Book of the Floor?"

"Yeah, yeah," said Mr. Darrow. "Wouldn't stop going on about it either."

He reached the top of the blowhole and heaved Luke out after him. They stood on top of the whale, its backbone stretching away from them like a hillside. The murky green lights of the warflies glimmered on the rubbish around them.

"*Damon's* my old boss," said Mr. Darrow. "A prize moron if ever there was one. I knew if he turned up before Max did, we really were stuffed. He'd hoover us all up without thinking. Maybe even do it on purpose, just to spite me! I had a *genius* idea for how to communicate with Max, but in order for it to work, I needed the whole Floor working together!"

Mr. Darrow started striding along the whale's spine. Luke scrambled to keep up.

"You see, Max wears these special earpieces in order to hear. I even put a radio in them once, for a bit of a laugh . . . and that got me thinking. If I could build a radio transmitter and a microphone, make it slow my voice down and set it to the right frequency, then I could use it to speak through Max's hearing aid and communicate with him! All the bits and pieces I needed were scattered across the floor—tidiness isn't exactly my strong point. I just needed to find the right parts."

The whale's spine sloped down toward the tail.

"So I told everyone to search the floor for me. I figured that a million hands are better than one, right?" He sighed. "Of course, those idiots all ended up forming into different tribes instead, squabbling over land and arguing with each other. I've spent the past eight weeks looking for all the parts myself, and just as I finally finished building the transmitter and microphone, Damon appeared and hoovered us all up!"

They came to the bottom of the whale's tail and jumped off.

"Now our only hope is to find a way out of here and communicate with Max. If not, then we really are doomed—you know where trash bags get taken, don't you? Junkyards! If we don't get out soon, we're all going to be crushed or incinerated! And the worst part is, I don't know where my equipment is—it's lost somewhere in this trash bag!"

Luke turned toward the darkness, his heart pounding. It all made sense to him. *This* was it. His chance to make up for everything he'd done. His one moment. His destiny.

"Then what are we waiting for?" said Luke. "We've got work to do!"

Mr. Darrow looked at him. "What do you mean?"

"We have to overthrow the Bin King!" said Luke. "Reunite the entire Floor! It's the only way we can save the world—I know it might sound impossible, but *nothing* is truly—"

"What are you talking about?" said Mr. Darrow. "We've done all that already. That's why I came to get you."

Luke's face fell. "What?"

"Ahem."

Luke turned round. Standing behind him was an enormous warfly, and hanging from its antenna was the Bin King, tied up and groaning. Next to him lay his fly riders, their arms held up in surrender as the Red Queen aimed a sword at their throats. And behind them stood the entire Floor: Reds, Greens and Blues, a million people, united at last.

"What took you so long?"

Luke looked up. Sitting on top of the warfly, looking extremely pleased with herself, was Ivy.

CHAPTER 34

Max tore into another trash bag and a heap of stinking gym socks tumbled out. Sasha tapped him on the shoulder.

"Anything?"

"Nothing!" cried Max.

It seemed like for every bag they opened, another twenty took its place. So far there'd been no sign of *anything* from Mr. Darrow's room—and they were running out of time.

"We have to hurry—Pitt could be here any moment!" said Max. "Even with Joy and the girls doing plan B, if we don't find the right bag soon, then—"

Sasha leapt back in shock. Max looked up—and his face drained. Mr. Pitt was standing at the door, holding a trash bag in a single clenched fist.

"Do you mean this bag?"

The builders had really done a number on the headmaster. His suit was torn, his tie was twisted, and he was covered in tea and jam.

"I bet you thought those builders would be able to hold me back. I'm afraid you underestimated me, boys."

He nodded to the door behind him. It was rattling and shaking as the builders tried to force their way in, but Mr. Pitt had pushed a metal bar though the handles.

"Did you really think I was going to let you stop me? After *everything* I've worked so hard for?"

Sasha made a leap for the bag, but Mr. Pitt whipped it away.

"Aha! Not so fast! Don't want to accidentally damage your precious *bag*, now, do we?"

Max gasped. Mr. Pitt still had no idea that there were people inside it. They had to keep him distracted.

"That bar's not going to hold the builders back forever, you know," Max said. "When they get in, they'll beat the stuffing out of you!"

Mr. Pitt laughed. "Oh, I don't need forever—just a few seconds."

He pushed over a heap of bags beside him. They tumbled to the floor, revealing a vast machine that had lain hidden beneath them. The machine was as tall and wide as the room, and at its front was a metal mouth filled with racks of jagged teeth.

"Like it?" said Mr. Pitt. "It's our new state-of-the-art

garbage disposal unit. It grinds everything down into a highly nutritious mulch, which can be added to school lunches to save money. It can get through a ton of rubbish in less than a minute!"

Mr. Pitt pulled a lever beside him, and the machine whirred to life. The room was filled with a noise so loud that Max's hearing aids blared with feedback. The jaws of the machine spun and twisted, faster and faster. Mr. Pitt held the bag above them.

"First I'm going to destroy this bag that you two care so much about," he said. "And then I'm going to expel both of you."

Max's eyes widened with horror. Mr. Pitt smiled at him.

"Remember, Max? *I always win.*"

Mr. Pitt was right—there was no way Max or Sasha could get the bag off him now. The floor people were doomed.

They needed a miracle.

CHAPTER 35

The Red Queen drew her sword and stepped forward.

"People of the Floor!" she cried. "Thanks to the Wise Man, we now know the whole truth—King Luke is no traitor!"

"That's right!" said Ivy. "He's just a bit of an idiot!"

Luke beamed. It was probably the biggest compliment Ivy had ever given him.

"Now to find a way out of this bag and protect our world, at any cost!" the Red Queen cried. "But first, let's finish what we started. Execute the Bin King and his fly riders!"

The crowd cheered. The Red Queen turned to the Bin King, her sword outstretched—

"*No!*" Luke leapt forward, blocking her. "We can't hurt anyone!"

He grabbed the Red Queen's sword and cut the Bin King down.

"We've got bigger things to think about now—if we want to get out of this bag alive, we have to let the Bin King go!"

The Bin King stared at Luke in shock. "You're ... you're not going to kill me, after everything I've done?"

Luke shook his head. "No. You're going to help us get out of here!"

He helped the Bin King to his feet.

"Get on your warflies and search every corner of this bag. Find a way for us to escape. Go!"

The Bin King nodded and scurried off with his fly riders. The Red Queen turned to Luke, her eyes blazing with fury.

"How dare you!"

"Sorry for taking your sword," said Luke nervously, handing it back, "but we don't have much time. Demon's making plans to destroy us as we speak. We need to organize an escape, and you're the only ruler left who people still trust. Can you take charge, Your Majesty?"

Some of the fire left the Red Queen's eyes. She sheathed her sword.

"Mmm. You're lucky to have friends like the Wise Man and Ivy. If it wasn't for them, I'd have left you to starve in that whale!"

She turned away and started giving orders to the

crowd. Ivy dropped down beside him. Luke scuffed his feet on the ground.

"Thanks," he said.

Ivy smiled. "What—for saving your life, even though you're a wiener?"

Luke blushed. "Yeah, fine. I was a total wiener."

Ivy patted him on the back. "Luke, you're the best wiener I know."

Mr. Darrow marched between them.

"Right! That's quite enough of that—we've got a transmitter and a microphone to find!" He pointed to the warfly that Ivy had just been sitting on. "Know how to fly that?"

Ivy's eyes lit up. "*Do I!*"

"She doesn't," said Luke nervously.

"That's good enough for me." Mr. Darrow started climbing up the bristles on the warfly's leg. "Fly low and slow. The transmitter's got a little flashing light on it. That's our only hope of finding it!"

Ivy leapt onto the warfly with a whoop of delight, grabbed the bristles on its head, and slowly lifted it from the ground. The warfly made a wobbling turn in the air and buzzed into the darkness. Soon the vast crowd of Floor people were far behind them, and Luke, Ivy and Mr. Darrow were alone.

"Wow," said Luke. "You're pretty good at this, Ivy."

"Don't be so surprised," Ivy muttered. "I'd be even better if I could see where I'm going, though! We need one of those green torches the fly riders were using earlier."

There was a sudden spark behind them, and the warfly lit up with a warm green glow. Mr. Darrow had found the torch and was holding it up, studying it.

"Mmm. Not bad work, you know. Must be done using a chemical reaction from that old bottle of bleach I put in the bin." He smiled. "Amazing what people can do when you leave them to it, isn't it?"

The warfly swerved, narrowly missing a huge building that loomed out of the dark.

"What was *that*?" said Luke.

Mr. Darrow grinned. "The Great Pyramid of Giza! Took me eight months to build, that one. Had to carve the interior chambers with a toothpick."

Luke was amazed. "You *made* that?"

Mr. Darrow nodded. "Course! I made them all—everything you can see. There's a whole lifetime of work in this trash bag."

Luke gazed around the darkness. All around them were vast intricate structures toppling over each other: boats and planes and palaces and monuments and dinosaurs and skyscrapers....

"Wow . . . you're a genius!" said Luke.

Mr. Darrow looked at him. "You think so?"

Luke nodded. Even in the dim glow of the green torch, Mr. Darrow couldn't possibly hide how pleased he looked.

"Well," he muttered. "About time."

"Luke?" said Ivy. "Could you come here for a moment, please?"

Luke sat beside her. Her face was worried.

"What's the matter?"

"This trash bag," she whispered. "It's *huge*. There's a whole Floor's worth of stuff in here. The transmitter could be buried under an inch of sand, or trapped beneath one of these enormous buildings . . . and even if we do manage to find it, it might not work."

Ivy glanced at Mr. Darrow, who was searching the darkness behind her with a single torch.

"I don't think he realizes how impossible this is. We're never going to find it in time. We have to think of some other way to—"

"*Down there!*"

Mr. Darrow was pointing below them. There, blinking in the sea of darkness, was a single pinprick of light.

"The transmitter! Quick—bring her down!"

Ivy nose-dived between the Statue of Liberty and the Colosseum, coming to a bumpy stop on the ground.

They jumped onto the sand, and there, just ahead of them, was a blinking white light.

"We did it! You brilliant, brilliant children!" Mr. Darrow said, laughing. "I don't know how it's possible, but we—"

He stopped. The light wasn't just blinking, it was coming toward them.

Luke held up the torch.

"Miss Binkles?"

The flea limped out of the darkness, filthy and bruised. She nuzzled Luke with a squeak and dropped something at his feet. It was the transmitter and microphone—beaten and bashed, but still working.

"I—I don't believe it," said Luke. "She found it! Miss Binkles, you're a hero!"

"You know this flea?" asked Mr. Darrow.

Luke hugged the flea tight, and Miss Binkles purred happily.

"She's my friend," said Luke. "And she's the best flea in the whole wide world."

So it was that one tiny boy, and the flea he had raised from a pupa, were able to save their world. They didn't know it at the time, but they were mere inches from death: held over the grinding wheels of a machine that was ready to destroy everything they knew. They were from two different species, and they had never spoken the same language, but they were friends. And sometimes, that's all you need to achieve the impossible.

No one saw it happen, of course. They were no bigger than ants. They were hidden in the darkness of a trash bag in a school basement.

The world is filled with millions of miracles that no one sees.

CHAPTER 36

Max's eyes flickered between Mr. Pitt and the bag in his hand. Sweat poured down his brow. The sound of the machine was overwhelming—Max had to keep his eyes locked on Mr. Pitt's lips to work out what he was saying.

"You know, boys," said Mr. Pitt with a sigh of pleasure, "it's moments like this that really make me appreciate being a headmaster."

Max and Sasha shared a glance. So long as they kept Mr. Pitt talking, they had a chance of saving the bag.

"I *never* wanted to run a school—I don't even like children! But the *power* . . . you should try it one day!"

The bag swung over the jaws of the machine.

"Once the governors have seen the Pitt Building, they'll put me on the board of governors too. I'll keep working all the way up to the top! Bigger schools, bigger boards—then, one day, I'll be the *national minister of education. Millions* of children under my control!"

He cackled and gave the bag another shake.

"But none of that matters to you, does it? All you care about is what's in this bag! A bag that means *nothing* to me!" He waved it at them mockingly. "Do you have any idea how much *power* that gives me, boys?"

Max froze. He had seen something behind Mr. Pitt— a tiny movement. The slightest change in the air.

A fly. A whole swarm of them. Dozens.

"As far as you two are concerned, I am your *GOD!*"

More and more flies were appearing. They'd made a hole in the side of the trash bag and were zooming out by the hundreds, their buzzing hidden by the sound of the whirring machine. Max couldn't believe his eyes— and with one glance, he could tell that Sasha couldn't, either. The only person who didn't realize was Mr. Pitt.

"Do you understand, boys?"

The flies were forming shapes in the air: one swarm became an arrow, pointed at Mr. Pitt's ears; the other was gathering to form a letter.

X

"DO YOU UNDERSTAND?"

Max stared at the flies in amazement. They were trying to communicate with him . . . and it was working. He understood completely.

He reached up to his hearing aid, pressed the pinprick button . . .

And a voice crackled out of his earpiece, clear and bright as day.

"*Max, it's Luke. Don't worry . . . we've got him now.*"

• • •

Luke sat on the highest warfly behind Mr. Pitt, the radio transmitter strapped to the bristle beside him. He was holding the microphone so tightly that the bones in his hands were almost visible.

"Luke, stop being such a wuss!" shouted Ivy.

Luke shot her a furious glance. She was still piloting the warfly, which was the main reason Luke was so terrified in the first place.

"Have you *seen* how high up we are? I can't even see the floor!"

Ivy smiled dreamily. "I know—wonderful, isn't it?"

"Quiet, you two!"

Mr. Darrow sat on a raised chair behind them, his eyes fixed on Max.

"I need to concentrate. I'm going to have to switch to Max's speed so we can help him!"

Luke frowned. "You can do that?"

"Course!" said Mr. Darrow. "Wasn't born a Floor person, was I? I can see things at both speeds if I want to. Makes me slow down a bit, that's all. Here we go!"

234

Mr. Darrow's eyes widened, his mouth hung open . . . and just like that, he fell into a trance. It was like he was fast asleep, but his eyes were wide open. Luke gulped—he was in charge now.

"Right, Max, listen up—here's the plan. . . ."

• • •

"MAX!"

Mr. Pitt was waving his arms, trying to get Max's attention. Max swallowed—he had to keep the headmaster distracted so he wouldn't see the flies.

"Er . . . yes, sir! Absolutely! You've won and we've lost and, er . . . so on."

Mr. Pitt smiled. "That's right! Maybe next time you'll think twice before trying to pull one over on me!"

Max kept one eye on Mr. Pitt while listening to Luke through the earpiece.

"Max, the Greens are on our side now. The rest of the Floor are inside the bag, waiting to escape."

The flies were forming a huge battalion in the air behind Mr. Pitt.

"We're going to distract Mr. Pitt," Luke explained. *"We need you and Sasha to grab the trash bag before it drops into the machine. Can you do that?"*

Max looked at Sasha. And with one look, he could tell

that Sasha understood. His face was glowing with excitement. The flies billowed up behind Mr. Pitt like a black wave, hanging over his head.

"Understand, boys?" said Mr. Pitt.

Max grinned. "Perfectly, sir."

"Clear as crystal," said Sasha.

"Oh crud," groaned Luke. *"Here goes."*

• • •

"Go, go, go!"

The flies swooped. Ivy led the squadron into a dive, bombing past Mr. Pitt's face at superfast speed.

"Fire!"

The warflies attacked, flinging round after round of catapult fire at Mr. Pitt's eyes. His face slowly twisted into a bellow of pain, and his free hand swung up . . .

"He's swatting!" cried Ivy. "Scramble!"

The warflies zipped away just as Mr. Pitt brought up his hand and punched himself square in the face. The warflies swarmed back round for another attack.

"Stage two!" Ivy shouted. "Bin King, are you ready?"

She turned to the warfly beside her. It was piloted by the Bin King. He seemed different somehow—his crown was gone. For the first time in his life, he looked happy.

"You're sure you want to do this?" said Luke.

The Bin King nodded. "This is the only way I can make up for everything I've done."

He nodded to Ivy, and Ivy nodded back. Luke saluted him.

"The Floor will never forget your sacrifice, Bin King. Everyone will remember your name!"

The Bin King smiled. "Thanks! But please, don't remember me as the Bin King. Remember my *real* name."

He tilted his warfly sharply in the air and shot forward, straight into Mr. Pitt's open mouth. He disappeared into the dark forever, punching the air with both hands.

"It's Terry!"

• • •

"AAAARRFGHGHGG!"

Mr. Pitt gagged and spluttered on the fly, reeling around like a broken toy. The trash bag fell from his grasp—

"Now, Max, now!" Luke shouted through the earpiece.

Max flew forward and grabbed the trash bag just before it hit the racks of grinding teeth—an inch more and it would have been destroyed. He nearly lost his balance and toppled into the machine himself, but Sasha dragged him back.

"*NOOOO!*"

Mr. Pitt's face was covered in welts and blisters from the warfly attacks. His eyes boiled with murderous rage. He tried to leap forward. . . .

But something was pulling him back. The tails of his suit were caught in the garbage disposal machine. He was being dragged backward, into the racks of grinding teeth. He reached for the lever, but it was too far.

"Boys! Quick!" he screamed. "Turn it off!"

Sasha smiled. "You'll be fine, Mr. Pitt . . . so long as you don't mind losing your suit. The question is: *Is it worth it?*"

Max and Sasha ran to the door with the trash bag, followed by Luke's warfly. Mr. Pitt bellowed with fury and heaved against the machine . . . until, with an almighty *RRRRRRRRIP,* the machine tore off his jacket, shirt and trousers and chewed them into highly nutritious mulch. The headmaster was left standing in his socks and underpants while the warflies swarmed round him, stinging every inch of his body.

Max tore the bar from the door handles, and the builders fell into the room, collapsing into a pile on the floor. Max and Sasha clambered over them before the men could get to their feet.

"There he is!" said the foreman, pointing at Pitt. "And he's naked! Get him!"

But Mr. Pitt wasn't going to stop now. He couldn't even feel pain anymore. He threw himself at the builders with a battle cry and sent them flying like bowling pins, charging after Max and Sasha as they ran up the stairs. . . .

• • •

Luke gasped. *"Max! He's right behind you!"*

Pitt was getting closer, and the warflies no longer seemed to be making any difference. Luke turned to Mr. Darrow for help, but he was still in his trance, his mouth gaping and his eyes gazing blankly ahead.

"Ivy, they're not going to make it!" cried Luke. "We have to get everyone out of the trash bag, now!"

He pointed to the bag in Max's arms. He could see the slit that the Greens had made to escape, and the Red Queen waiting beside it. The rest of the Floor were organized into a colossal human chain behind her so that no one would be left behind.

"It's too dangerous!" said Ivy. "We'll never be able to carry people out with the bag moving around like that— we'll drop them!"

"Then . . . what do we do?" cried Luke.

Ivy looked ahead, and smiled. Max and Sasha had reached the top of the staircase and were running into the foyer.

"I think these two might already have it covered," she said.

• • •

Max and Sasha burst into the foyer.

"*Girls, quick!*" cried Max. "*Time for plan B!*"

Above them, the girls stood on the X-shaped walk-way, armed with bottles of glue and buckets of glitter. Max and Sasha jumped out of the way just as Mr. Pitt burst through the doors.

"*Now!*" cried Joy.

The girls let rip. Within seconds, Mr. Pitt was doused from head to toe with glue and smashed with twenty bucketfuls of bright red, blue and green glitter. Choked and blinded, he swung his arms through the glittery cloud and roared like a stunned bear. Sasha grabbed Max by the arm.

"Quick! This way!"

They flew up another set of stairs to the next floor, but Mr. Pitt had heard Sasha shout. He clawed the glit-ter from his eyes and threw himself after them, his arms stretched toward the bag. . . .

• • •

"It didn't work!" cried Luke. "He's going to catch them! Mr. Darrow, *wake up!*"

Luke shook Mr. Darrow as hard as he could, but it was no use. The clouds of glitter filled the air around them like fireworks, exploding in colossal plumes of red, green and blue. Mr. Darrow even had a faint smile on his lips....

Then he snapped out of the trance.

"Tell Max to get on that walkway, now!" he said. "Ivy, how do you feel about causing as much damage as possible?"

"Great," she said.

"Thought so." Mr. Darrow pointed above them. "Just do everything I say...."

• • •

Max was almost at the top of the stairs. Sasha flung open a door and held it open for the girls as they fled.

"Max, quick!" he cried, waving an arm. "Through here!"

"*No, Max, get on the walkway!*" came Luke's voice.

Max skidded on his heels and tore down the X-shaped walkway instead. There was a door on the other side—

241

he had no idea what was behind it, but he had to trust Luke. He grabbed the door handle, wrenched at it—but the door was locked.

"WRONG CHOICE, MAX!"

Max spun round . . . straight into Mr. Pitt.

"DID YOU REALLY THINK YOU COULD DEFEAT ME?"

The headmaster shoved Max backward and whipped the bag out of his hands. In one go, he threw the bag to the floor, lifted up one foot . . .

"No!" cried Max.

"*NO!*" cried Luke.

. . . and stamped on it.

The *crunch* of the bag was sickening. Pitt stamped on it again, and again, and again, and again. He jumped on the bag in a frenzy of rage until it was completely flattened.

"I WILL NOT BE BEATEN BY A DEAF BOY AND A *UNICORN!*"

"It's a Sparkle Pony."

Mr. Pitt swung round. Sasha stood on the other end of the walkway in his purple onesie, a mysterious smile on his face.

"I'm not a unicorn. I'm a Sparkle Pony. They're a completely different species. Many thousands of years ago, there was a beautiful horse goddess called Glimmer, who—"

"What on *earth* are you on about?" snapped Mr. Pitt.

Sasha smiled. "Of course you don't care about the details. And *that's* why you'll never win, Mr. Pitt: because you'll never understand that details matter."

"For example," said Max, getting back to his feet, "that's not actually our trash bag."

Mr. Pitt looked down at the bag—Max was right. *This* bag was filled with old milk from last term. Mr. Pitt's legs were now covered in cheesy green yogurt.

"*Our* trash bag is over there," said Max.

He pointed to Joy, who was holding up the correct bag and waving.

"We switched them when we came in the foyer. We thought someone like you wouldn't notice the difference."

Mr. Pitt growled. "Why, you little . . ."

He made to grab Max—but stopped. There was a fly buzzing in front of his face. Mr. Pitt jerked his head back, expecting another sting, but none came. He focused on the fly . . . and his eyes boggled.

There were tiny people riding on the fly's back. They were all waving at him.

One of them was Mr. Darrow.

Max put one hand to his hearing aid. "Mr. Pitt, they're asking if you could hold your hand out, please?"

Mr. Pitt held out his hand, dumbstruck. The fly deposited something into the center of his palm, then quickly buzzed away. Mr. Pitt held it up.

It was a single screw.

The walkway supports around him began to creak. It might have only been one screw, but without it the poorly built walkway wasn't strong enough to hold itself up. One by one, the supports started to pull away from the walls. Mr. Pitt didn't notice—he was too busy staring dumbfounded at the fly that was buzzing away.

"RUN, MAX!" cried Sasha.

Max, Sasha and the girls ran outside just as the walkway snapped free from its supports and cracks appeared in the glass ceiling. It was the butterfly effect—one tiny change was enough to destroy everything Mr. Pitt had built, and bring him down with it.

In many ways, the odds of the plan coming together so perfectly were astronomical—impossible, even. It was nothing short of a miracle.

But then, we all know about miracles by now.

CHAPTER 37

Max, Sasha and Joy sat in the bushes with the trash bag between them. They watched as Mr. Pitt was led away by the police, kicking and shouting. Sasha tapped Max on the shoulder.

"Do you reckon he'll go to jail?"

Max shrugged. "Probably not. But I don't think he'll ever be a headmaster again."

The governors had turned up shortly after the Pitt Building collapsed, and found Mr. Pitt in the car park in his underwear. He was covered in blisters and old milk, and was raving about a tiny janitor riding a fly. By the time the builders had reappeared saying something about the school being bankrupt, the governors had heard all they needed.

"And what about the school?" said Joy. "Is St. Goliath's going to close down now?"

Sasha patted her on the back. "They'll think of

something, Joy. In the meantime, we need to get you back to the boardinghouse. The governors will be checking the rest of the school soon!"

Joy groaned. "Can't I come with you?"

Sasha shook his head. "Max and I have something important to do, and—"

Max put a hand on his shoulder.

"Let her come. We couldn't have done any of this without her."

They made their way to Mr. Darrow's potting shed, and Max carefully placed the trash bag on the table. He reached into it and found the microscope goggles. He pulled them on and focused the lenses so he could see thousands of tiny faces peeking through the slit in the plastic.

"You can come out now," said Max. "This is it—your new home!"

Max knew the floor people wouldn't understand his words, but they understood enough. They started pouring out of the bag and filling the trays on the table. Max smiled.

"We did it! The floor people finally have somewhere safe to live."

Max felt another tap on his shoulder.

"But, Max," said Sasha, "what about you? You're not still going to be expelled, are you?"

Joy gripped Max's arm. "We won't let them do it, Max! We'll tell the governors what happened—they're *bound* to let you stay!"

Max shared a glance with Sasha. They both wished Joy were right, but they knew the truth. People rarely believe children. How could they explain everything that had happened—all the damage they had caused to the school—without giving away the truth about the tiny world?

"It doesn't matter, Joy," said Max. "Mr. Darrow's coming back, remember? When he does, we can work something out together and—"

"Max."

Max froze. There was a voice in his ear that he hadn't expected to hear. He looked at the warfly hovering in front of him. . . .

And his heart swelled.

Standing beside Luke was a girl with red hair, and standing beside her was Mr. Darrow.

• • •

"Yes, it's me."

Mr. Darrow stood holding the microphone. Max stared back at him, still gobsmacked.

"I've been here all along, and I've been watching you. You did brilliantly, Max—I'm so proud of you."

It took a while for the words to register with Max, and for the blush to spread across his cheeks like a sunset. Mr. Darrow cleared his throat.

"I've been trying to find you for a long time now. I needed you to help me get back to normal size. But now . . ."

Mr. Darrow looked at Luke and Ivy beside him and gave them a warm smile.

"Now I don't want to go back. There's nothing for me in the big world anymore. No wife, no family—just my models. I used to think they were everything, but I was wrong. They're nothing compared with being around good people. The only thing I don't want to leave behind is you."

Mr. Darrow looked up at Max and sighed.

"Saying goodbye to you will be very, very hard, Max. But we don't have to say goodbye. Not if you don't want to."

Max stared at Mr. Darrow in confusion.

"Look inside the trash bag—in the trouser pocket. There's something you should see."

• • •

Max reached inside the trash bag and pulled out a tiny glass bottle.

"That's the serum that made all this happen," said Mr. Darrow. "The secret ingredient that made me shrink to this size. I spent twenty years looking for it, and now it's all gone . . . except for one drop."

Max looked inside the bottle.

"It's your choice, Max," said Mr. Darrow. "If you want to stay behind, I understand completely. But if you want to join us, then drink that drop. It'll be enough to shrink you."

Max looked at Mr. Darrow with shock.

"I know how lonely you are," said Mr. Darrow. "I know how miserable you were at your aunt's. You never told me about it, but I could see it in your eyes. It was one of the reasons I agreed to teach you—I wanted to help. Of course, in the end it was you who helped me."

Max looked at the serum. He thought about what the rest of his life would be like now—being expelled, living with his great-aunt Meredith on the other side of the country. . . .

"If you stay with us, you'll be tiny—but you'll be hidden, too. You'll be safe. We'll have enough time to work out a way to safely return to normal size together. But it's your choice."

Max felt a hand on his shoulder.

"Hey, is that *Mr. Darrow* on that fly?"

Sasha stood behind Max, grinning with amazement.

"No way! What's he saying?"

Max swallowed.

"Er . . . just explaining how he got so small."

Sasha smiled. "Wow! You'll have to tell me all about it! Look, I might have to go back to the boardinghouse. Joy's exhausted."

He nodded to his sister, who was slumped against his leg, her eyes drooping.

"Are you coming?"

Max looked at Sasha—the nicest, kindest person he had ever met. His new friend. Then he turned to Mr. Darrow—the man who'd taught him everything he knew. The closest thing Max had ever had to a father. Max had never had to make a choice like this before. He looked between them, his face torn.

"I . . . I . . ."

Then Max saw Luke and the red-haired girl standing beside Mr. Darrow. He saw the millions of tiny people below them, gazing up at him on the table, all of them relying on him to survive. And he knew exactly what he had to do.

"No, Sasha," he said quietly. "I'm not coming. Sorry."

"OK—I'll meet you at the boardinghouse later and—"

"No," said Max. "I mean . . . I'm staying here. With the floor people."

Sasha frowned. "What? Max, you can't live in a shed, that's *weird*."

"Not like that," said Max. "I mean *live with* the floor people—in their world. Mr. Darrow says there's a way to do it. I'm going to shrink to their size and live with them."

Sasha still didn't understand. "Max, you're not making any sense! If you do that, I can't go with you—I've got Joy to look after!"

"I know you can't," said Max.

He had to watch the realization dawn across Sasha's face. It broke his heart.

"What's going on?"

Joy snapped awake, gazing up at them through half-shut eyes. Sasha swallowed hard and quickly regained his composure. He rubbed her head with a reassuring smile.

"Hey, Joy, can you wait outside for a second?"

She nodded sleepily. "OK. I'll go get some of Mr. Darrow's carrots for the girls. We've been taking them all year."

"I knew it!" snapped Mr. Darrow.

Joy stepped outside, and Sasha closed the door.

"Max, you can't go. You can't just leave everything behind."

"We *both* know I'm going to be expelled," said Max. "I'm not like you—I don't have family I belong to. I don't have anyone who needs me. The only people who have ever needed me are . . . *them.*"

He held out his hand to the millions of tiny faces spread across the seedling trays.

"The floor people will never survive here without my help—they've never even left the bedroom! Mr. Darrow can't do it all on his own. I've spent my whole life trying to avoid people, and I don't want to do it anymore. I want to help them. They *need* me, Sasha."

Sasha winced. "*I* need you, Max."

Sasha pulled the hood tighter around his face, but he couldn't hide the tears that were making tiny snowflakes on the dusty floor. Max put a hand on his shoulder.

"It's not for forever, Sasha. I'm going to come back. Mr. Darrow and I are going to find a way to return to normal size. Until then, I'll be right here—we can talk anytime you want!"

Sasha looked up, his eyes wet. "*How?*"

Max looked at him for a while. Then, slowly, he reached up and took out his hearing aids. They whistled loudly with feedback . . . and then his world was silent. He knew he would have to rely on lip-reading alone from now on.

Max handed them over. When he spoke, all he could hear was his own voice deep in his chest, where his heart was.

"Take them. Listen for me—I'll be right here."

Sasha took the hearing aids and beamed.

"I'll come every day—twice a day, even! Anything you need, just ask!"

Max put a hand on Sasha's shoulder. "Thank you, Sasha."

He paused. He hoped that what he was going to say next would come out right.

"Not just for the help, for everything. For being kind to me. For showing me what I can do. For being my friend. You're the nicest guy I've ever met—and you shouldn't let your parents leave you here. You should tell them you want to go home at the holidays and see your old friends. Joy deserves better, and so do—"

Before Max could finish the sentence, Sasha grabbed him and hugged him tight. Max stopped talking—he didn't need to say anything more.

"Bye, Max."

"Goodbye, Sasha."

They reached out and crossed fingers—X. Then Max stepped back and took a deep breath.

"Oh well," he said. "Here goes nothing. . . ."

He held the bottle high above him, and let the last remaining drop of serum land on his tongue.

Max felt the change in his stomach first. It was like all his insides were getting smaller at the same time. The breath squeezed out of his lungs, and the muscles round his heart tensed and tightened. His legs gave way and he fell onto the table, trembling. Sasha was in front of him in seconds, his face concerned.

"Max! Are you OK?"

Sasha's face was growing right in front of him. The shed was getting bigger and bigger too, and suddenly it felt like he was falling into himself. His T-shirt became bigger and heavier and billowed up around him like a three-ring circus. Before he knew it, Sasha's face was disappearing faster and faster above him, his movements slowing and grinding like a film in slow motion. . . .

• • •

And then Max was alone.

His T-shirt was spread like a landscape around him, as far as he could see. Sasha loomed over him, his face flickering with the tiniest movements, like a field of grass in the wind.

Max sat up. The entire Floor was running toward him, their lips all forming the same words.

"The Great One!"

Max had never seen so many people so happy to see him before. And right at the very front . . .

"MR. DARROW!"

Max leapt to his feet and ran toward him. But to his confusion, everyone started blushing and turning away. Everyone except for Ivy, who was almost senseless with laughter. Max suddenly caught sight of Luke, waving his hands to get his attention.

"Max, your clothes!"

Max looked down, and yelped. He was completely naked. He clapped a hand over his privates and glared at Mr. Darrow.

"Oh yeah!" muttered Mr. Darrow. "The serum doesn't shrink your clothes. Sorry—should have mentioned that."

Someone quickly handed Max a spare fly rider's outfit and he got dressed while a million people faced the other way. Even Sasha hid his eyes. When Max was finally ready—and Ivy had stopped laughing—the Floor people fell to their knees in front of him.

"Welcome back, Great One!" cried a Blue. "We never stopped believing in you!"

"Lead us, Great One, please!"

"Remember when you found my keys?"

Max waved them all quiet—he wasn't used to so many people talking to him at once. He cleared his throat and hoped he could make them understand him.

"Sorry," he explained, his voice still booming in his chest. "I'm not really the Great One. That was, well . . . a lie." He pointed at Mr. Darrow. "*That's* the Great One, if you're interested."

The entire Floor shuffled round on their knees to face Mr. Darrow.

"Lead us, Great One!"

"We always believed in you!"

Mr. Darrow grumbled and tried to bat them all away, without success.

Max felt a tap on his shoulder. He turned around and saw a face he recognized instantly. A face he knew like the back of his hand.

"It's you!" said Luke.

Max smiled. "It's *you!*"

Luke held out his fingers in an X, but Max hugged him instead. Luke stepped back and stared him up and down in disbelief.

"I . . . I don't believe it. I'm *taller* than you."

Mr. Darrow placed a hand on Max's shoulder.

"Thank you for coming, Max," he said. "And make sure you thank your friend, too. We couldn't have done any of this without him."

They looked up at the sky. Sasha stood over them, gazing down at the world. From here, you could see the exact point where happiness and sadness met in his eyes.

"You'll be able to hear everything he says, you know," said Mr. Darrow. "You and I can hear things at his speed. I'll teach you how to do it. We're going to need a lot of help from Sasha from now on. . . ."

"Like what?"

Mr. Darrow laughed, and gave him a playful hug.

"We've got plenty of time to talk about that, Max. For now, let's get this lot moving."

He pointed to the Floor people around them. They were forming lines to the warflies, and Luke and Ivy and the Red Queen were taking charge, explaining plans and showing people where to go. Everyone was helping each other.

"*Moving?*" said Max. "Where to?"

Mr. Darrow gave him a look.

"Where do you think?" he said. "*Paradise*, of course."

• • •

Sasha watched as Max was lost among the millions of tiny people clustering around him. He felt like his heart was ready to burst, but he wasn't sad. He'd never seen Max so happy before.

"Sasha?"

Joy was standing at the door, rubbing her eyes.

"Where's Max?"

Sasha smiled. He picked up the microscope goggles and gently put them over her head.

"See for yourself."

Joy gasped with amazement. The whole world was transformed around her. The shed had become a place of wonders.

"The flies!"

They were leaving the shed. One by one they buzzed through the air, laden with families and friends and people who just moments ago had been strangers. The green glow of their torches lit their way like a string of fairy lamps. They flew out the shed door, carrying a million people a handful at a time to their new home.

They were landing in the vegetable patch.

CHAPTER 38

Max was in paradise.

Actually, it was Mr. Darrow's vegetable patch. But to the people of the Floor, it was a place where food grew out of the ground, and water sometimes fell from the sky. It was the most incredible place they could possibly imagine.

Sure, it was hard going sometimes—most of them had never experienced "night" before, or this thing called "Winter" that was going to come and shake things up—but with Max's help and advice, and Mr. Darrow's amazing inventions, the Floor people had learned to adapt. Working together, they had turned the vegetable patch into something wonderful.

"Max!"

Max's eye was caught by something in the distance—Luke, waving at him. Luke sat on top of Miss Binkles, who was hopping alongside a tick she'd recently be-friended.

"Hi, guys!" said Max. "Check it out—I'm almost done."

He pointed to his latest creation: a hut carved into a cabbage stalk. His skills as a model-maker had led to him becoming one of the most sought-after architects in the vegetable patch. His recent Leek Skyscraper had won awards. The rest of the Floor lived in Mr. Darrow's models, tucked among the vegetables: the Taj Mahal, Sydney Opera House, the Houses of Parliament . . .

"I'm giving it to Mr. Darrow," he said. "To thank him for making my new hearing aids!"

Max pointed to them. They were much bigger than his last ones, but thanks to Mr. Darrow's ingenuity, they worked just as well. It had taken a little while for the Floor people to learn how to talk to Max properly, but then, they were learning a *lot* about talking to one an-other nowadays. And of course, Luke was there to help them every step of the way.

"They're even better than my last ones," Max ex-plained. "And just in time, too—Sasha's going back to America in half term!"

True to his word, Sasha had turned up twice a day to check that the Floor people were OK. Max and Mr. Darrow had explained their plan to him—that when he went back home for the holidays, he needed to

persuade his parents to visit a certain town in Massachusetts, a certain town with a certain abandoned museum, with a certain basement that Mr. Darrow had once explored—

"*Look out below!*"

Luke screamed as Ivy landed beside them with a thump. She was wearing a pair of handmade moth wings and grinning like a lunatic.

"Did you see that? It was my highest one yet!"

Ivy had recently made herself head explorer, and volunteered for every mission to fly round the school grounds and find things for Mr. Darrow. She'd also started jumping off the warflies midflight so she could paraglide her way back down to the ground on her homemade wings, and terrify Luke in the process.

"Come on!" she said. "We're almost late—the big meeting's about to start in Potato Hall. We're going to vote on how to make peace with the slugs, remember?"

She pointed to the crowds of Reds, Greens and Blues heading toward the meeting on a centipede bus. Max put down his tools and dusted off his hands.

"Sure! I'll go tell Mr. Darrow."

Ivy snorted. "Ha! Good luck—he's in his workshop."

Max groaned. "*Again?*"

"He barely leaves," said Luke. "All day long on the same project of his, work, work, work..."

Ivy shook her head. "I don't get it. There's a whole amazing world right here in front of him, and he's still focusing on the small stuff!"

Max shrugged. "You can't underestimate the small stuff, Ivy—everything's small to something else."

Luke gawped. "Even Sasha?"

"Of course."

"But he's over five feet tall!"

"That's not *that* tall where I come from."

"Were *you* taller than him?"

Max blushed. "Er . . . yeah, I think so."

The three friends jumped on Miss Binkles's back, and together they went to build their world.

• • •

Mr. Darrow was also building a world.

He was in the empty glass bottle: his workshop. There was a chair and a desk inside it, and nothing else.

On the desk lay a single scrap of leaf. Collected inside was all the serum he had painstakingly scraped off the glass bottle over many hours. There was barely anything left—one hundredth of a single drop. Not enough for him to experiment on. Not enough to see if he and Max could reverse the transformation and go back to normal size. Of course, when Sasha returned from holiday, he should have more serum with him. They had plenty of time to find their way home.

Until then, Mr. Darrow had a lifelong dream to fulfill.

He took a bristle from a courgette plant, picked up the single microscopic droplet of serum in front of him, and held it over his latest creation.

It was a tiny model of paradise, no bigger than a grain of sand.

It's hard for us to understand quite how small it was. It's even harder for us to understand how tiny—how *infinitesimally small*—the people who lived inside it would be. You couldn't have seen them with your own eyes, even if you tried.

But then, the world is filled with miracles that no one sees.

"Well then," said Mr. Darrow, "here goes nothing."

ACKNOWLEDGMENTS

Until the age of four I had glue ear (a buildup of thick fluid in the middle ear), which made me mildly deaf. Before I was diagnosed, no one could understand why I kept ignoring people and got so frustrated whenever anyone tried to talk to me. Surgeons fixed the problem by putting little tubes called grommets in my ears. After that, my mum ran me a bath and I freaked out because the taps were too loud.

Before I started writing *Max & the Millions*, that was my only experience of deafness. Even now I hardly know anything. There are several people who have taught me a lot while writing this book and helped me understand what it means for someone like Max to be deaf in a hearing world. I owe them a great deal of thanks.

They are: James Martin, who read an early draft and gave me invaluable advice; Fiona Gray and all the staff and children at James Wolfe Centre for the Deaf in

Greenwich, England, for sharing so many of their experiences with me; Lindsey Frodsham at the National Deaf Children's Society (ndcs.org.uk) for her help and advice; and Carol Lynn Kearney, senior adjunct in the Department of Communication Sciences and Disorders at Adelphi University, for her suggestions. Without them, this book would be rubbish.

The lines Mr. Darrow recites to Max are from the poem "Auguries of Innocence" by William Blake.

Finally, if you think Mr. Darrow's tiny hand-carved houses sound unrealistic, go online and check out the work of microartist Willard Wigan. From single grains of sand, he carves incredible sculptures so small they can't be seen with the naked eye.

Take care of the small things—they make up the universe.

ABOUT THE AUTHOR

Ross Montgomery has worked as a pig farmer, a postman, and a primary school teacher, so writing books was the next logical step. He spent his childhood reading everything he could get his hands on, from Jacqueline Wilson to comic books, and it taught him pretty much everything that's worth knowing. If you looked through his pockets, you'd find empty potato chip packets, lists of things to do, and a bottle of that stuff you put on your nails to stop you from biting them. He lives in London with his girlfriend, a cat called Fun Bobby, and a cactus on every available surface.